The Come Back

By Carolyn Wells

Originally published in 1921

The Come Back

© 2013 Resurrected Press
www.ResurrectedPress.com

Published by Resurrected Press

This classic book was handcrafted by Resurrected Press. Resurrected Press is dedicated to bringing high quality classic books back to the readers who enjoy them. These are not scanned versions of the originals, but, rather, quality checked and edited books meant to be enjoyed!

Please visit ResurrectedPress.com to view our entire catalogue!

ISBN 13: 978-1-937022-66-2

Printed in the United States of America

RESURRECTED PRESS CLASSIC MYSTERY CATALOGUE

Journeys into Mystery
Travel and Mystery in a More Elegant Time

The Edwardian Detectives
Literary Sleuths of the Edwardian Era

Gems of Mystery
Lost Jewels from a More Elegant Age

Anne Austin
One Drop of Blood
The Black Pigeon
Murder at Bridge

E. C. Bentley
Trent's Last Case: The Woman in Black

Ernest Bramah
Max Carrados Resurrected:
The Detective Stories of Max Carrados

Agatha Christie
The Secret Adversary
The Mysterious Affair at Styles

Octavus Roy Cohen
Midnight

Freeman Wills Croft
The Ponson Case
The Pit Prop Syndicate

J. S. Fletcher

The Herapath Property
The Rayner-Slade Amalgamation
The Chestermarke Instinct
The Paradise Mystery
Dead Men's Money
The Middle of Things
Ravensdene Court
Scarhaven Keep
The Orange-Yellow Diamond
The Middle Temple Murder
The Tallyrand Maxim
The Borough Treasurer
In the Mayor's Parlour
The Saftey Pin

R. Austin Freeman

*The Mystery of 31 New Inn from the Dr. Thorndyke
Series*
*John Thorndyke's Cases from the Dr. Thorndyke
Series*
The Red Thumb Mark from The Dr. Thorndyke Series
The Eye of Osiris from The Dr. Thorndyke Series
A Silent Witness from the Dr. John Thorndyke Series
The Cat's Eye from the Dr. John Thorndyke Series
*Helen Vardon's Confession: A Dr. John Thorndyke
Story*
As a Thief in the Night: A Dr. John Thorndyke Story
*Mr. Pottermack's Oversight: A Dr. John Thorndyke
Story*
*Dr. Thorndyke Intervenes: A Dr. John Thorndyke
Story*
The Singing Bone: The Adventures of Dr. Thorndyke
The Stoneware Monkey: A Dr. John Thorndyke Story
*The Great Portrait Mystery, and Other Stories: A
Collection of Dr. John Thorndyke and Other Stories*
The Penrose Mystery: A Dr. John Thorndyke Story
The Uttermost Farthing: A Savant's Vendetta

Arthur Griffiths
The Passenger From Calais
The Rome Express

Fergus Hume
The Mystery of a Hansom Cab
The Green Mummy
The Silent House
The Secret Passage

Edgar Jepson
The Loudwater Mystery

A. E. W. Mason
At the Villa Rose

A. A. Milne
The Red House Mystery

Baroness Emma Orczy
The Old Man in the Corner

Edgar Allan Poe
The Detective Stories of Edgar Allan Poe

Arthur J. Rees
The Hampstead Mystery
The Shrieking Pit
The Hand In The Dark
The Moon Rock
The Mystery of the Downs

Mary Roberts Rinehart
Sight Unseen and The Confession

Dorothy L. Sayers
Whose Body?

Sir William Magnay
The Hunt Ball Mystery

Mabel and Paul Thorne
The Sheridan Road Mystery

Louis Tracy
The Strange Case of Mortimer Fenley
The Albert Gate Mystery
The Bartlett Mystery
The Postmaster's Daughter
The House of Peril
The Sandling Case: What Would You Have Done?

Charles Edmonds Walk
The Paternoster Ruby

John R. Watson
The Mystery of the Downs
The Hampstead Mystery

Edgar Wallace
The Daffodil Mystery
The Crimson Circle

Carolyn Wells
Vicky Van
The Man Who Fell Through the Earth
In the Onyx Lobby
Raspberry Jam
The Clue
The Room with the Tassels
The Vanishing of Betty Varian
The Mystery Girl
The White Alley
The Curved Blades
Anybody but Anne

The Bride of a Moment
Faulkner's Folly
The Diamond Pin
The Gold Bag
The Mystery of the Sycamore
The Come Back

Raoul Whitfield
Death in a Bowl

And much more!
Visit ResurrectedPress.com
for our complete catalogue

FOREWORD

A number of Carolyn Wells' books involve a supernatural element, with legends of ghosts or haunted mansions serving as a backdrop for the mystery, but in none of them is the supernatural as central to the story as spiritualism is in *The Come Back*.

Spiritualism was a belief on the part of many people through much of the nineteenth and early twentieth century that the spirits of the dead could be contacted through certain individuals known as *mediums* during a *séance*, a ritual, usually carried out in a darkened room, often with the participants sitting around a table holding hands.

Throughout this period, the strength of the belief in spiritualism ebbed and waned, but at its peak adherents numbered in the millions on both sides of the Atlantic. The movement was particularly strong after both the Civil War and the First World War when grieving relatives sought to make contact with loved ones who had died in those conflicts.

While even the most confirmed believers acknowledged that many of the *mediums* were fakes or charlatans, their faith that there were at least some true experiences was unshakeable. A number of prominent scientists and intellectuals were believers in spiritualism or at least kept an open mind, including physicist William Crookes, biologist Alfred Russell Wallace, and Nobel prize winner Charles Richet. Author and physician Sir Arthur Conan Doyle became interested after losing his son in the war.

The early 1920's, the period when *The Come Back* was written, was one of the peaks in the popularity of the movement, and most of the audience of the book would have been familiar with the topic, no matter what their personal beliefs. And *séances* were a regular feature of many mysteries of the period.

Along with spiritualism, the Ouija board was another manifestation of the public's interest in the paranormal at the time. The Ouija board consisted of a heart shaped pointer which could be moved over a board on which letters, numbers, and the words "yes" and "no" were displayed. Two or more people would rest their fingers lightly on the pointer which would seem to move under its own volition to answer questions posed by the participants, supposedly under control of the spirits. The Ouija was both a popular parlour game and a tool of more serious investigators. Of course, it was also open to manipulation by participants who did not want to play "fair."

For those readers unfamiliar with Pennington Wise, the detective appears in a number of mysteries by Wells, always accompanied by his unusual assistant, Zisi, a young woman of indeterminate age and exotic appearance. Zizi often acts as a comedic foil to the more serious Wise, though it often she who discovers the critical clue. Wells' style was to use her professional detectives in a supporting role, with the bulk of the detection being done by friends or relatives of the victim. Indeed, her other reoccurring detective, Fleming Stone, usually doesn't appear until the last three or four chapters of the book, when he makes a brief tour of the crime scene, finds the vital clue, and then reveals the solution in the last chapter. Wells is much more concerned with the interaction of the various characters than the actual detection.

On a literary note, the murderer is revealed with the phrase "Thou art the man." This phrase is the title of a story by Edgar Allan Poe, who many credit with inventing the detective story. In the story, the murderer goes to great lengths to establish an alibi or himself while implicating another person, certainly the first use of this device.

Carolyn Wells was an extremely popular author in her time, writing over a hundred mysteries over a span of about thirty years in addition to dozens of other works of humor and poetry. Her mysteries provide not only a puzzle for the reader, but a glimpse into the society of the era. It is with great pleasure that Resurrected Press brings you this new edition of *The Come Back*.

About the Author

Carolyn Wells, June 18, 1862 March 26, 1942 was an American writer and poet. She was best known for her books of poetry and humor until around 1910 she read one of Anna Katherine Green's mysteries and took up the genre. Many of her mysteries featured the detective Fleming Stone. She was married to Hadwin Houghton, heir to the Houghton-Mifflin publishing company. She was a collector of poetry by other authors, and, upon her death, she bequeathed her collection of the works of Walt Witman to the Library of Congress.

Greg Fowlkes
Editor-In-Chief
Resurrected Press
www.ResurrectedPress.com

TABLE OF CONTENTS

CHAPTER 1: THE PROPHECY...1

CHAPTER 2: THE LABRADOR WILD.....................................13

CHAPTER 3: THE SNOWSTORM...25

CHAPTER 4: THE PROPHECY RECALLED.........................37

CHAPTER 5: MADAME PARLATO...49

CHAPTER 6: STRANGE REVELATIONS.............................61

CHAPTER 7: THE TOBACCO POUCH....................................73

CHAPTER 8: BLAIR KNOWS..85

CHAPTER 9: INVESTIGATION...97

CHAPTER 10: EVIDENCE...109

CHAPTER 11: CARLOTTA AND THE BOARD...................121

CHAPTER 12: WISE AND ZIZI...133

CHAPTER 13: "LABRADOR LUCK".....................................145

CHAPTER 14: A PROPHECY FULFILLED............................157

CHAPTER 15: AN INTERVIEW...169

CHAPTER 16: ZIZI'S OPPORTUNITY..................................181

CHAPTER 17: THE HEART HELPER.....................................193

CHAPTER 18: THE CONFESSION...205

CHAPTER 1: THE PROPHECY

Even when Peter Crane was a baby boy, with eyes the color of the chicory flowers that grow by the wayside along New England roads, and hair that rivaled the Blessed Damosel's in being "yellow like ripe corn," he was of an adventurous disposition.

His innocent face was never so devoid of guile, his winning smile never so cherubic as when he remarked that he would "jes' run froo the front gate a minyit," and the next instant he was out of sight. Far afield his roving spirit led him, and much scurrying was needed on the part of nurse or mother to bring him back.

At four he achieved a pair of most wonderful russet-topped boots,—aye, even with straps to lift himself over a fence, if a fence came his way. And these so accentuated and emphasized his world-faring inclinations that he came to be known as Peter Boots.

The name stuck, for Peter was always ready to boot it, and all through his school and college days he led his willing mates wherever he listed. He stalked forth and they followed; and, as he stopped not for brake and stayed not for stone, the boys who eagerly trailed Peter Boots became sturdy fellows.

And now, at twenty-seven, Peter Boots was more than sturdy. He was tall and big and strong, and the love of adventure, the dare-devil spirit of exploration still shone in his chicory blue eyes, and his indomitable will power was evident in his straight fine mouth and firm jaw.

He had traveled some, even before the war, and now, comfortably settled in his chosen niche and civilly engineering his way through the world, he grasped at vacation seasons because they offered him a chance to don his boots and be off.

This year he had a grand plan,—its objective point being nothing short of Labrador.

He had read many books of the North lands, but a delightful chance meeting with a doctor who lived up there gave him a sudden impetus to go and explore a little for himself. His decision to start was instantaneous, and there remained but to make the necessary arrangements.

For Peter Boots these arrangements consisted merely in getting two congenial companions, and to them he left all minor details of paraphernalia and equipment. Not that Peter was lazy or inclined to shift his burdens to others' shoulders, but he was so engrossed with the itinerary and calculations of distance, climate and season that he had no time to engage guides or buy camp outfits.

But the two men he picked,—and who jumped at the chance,—were more than willing and perfectly capable of all this, and so all details of the expedition were carefully looked after.

There had been opposition, of course. Peter's parents were emphatically unwilling to let their only son run dangers, all the more fearsome because only vaguely apprehended.

But their big boy smiled genially at them and went on with his calculations.

His sister, too, pretty Julie, besought him not to go. "You'll get lost in the ice," she wailed, "and never come back to me—and Carly."

Now Carly,—otherwise Miss Carlotta Harper—was a disturbing element in the even tenor of Peter's life, and of late her disturbance had attained such importance that tucked away in a corner of his big, happy heart was a cozy, cuddly little notion that when he came back from Labrador he would take her to embark with him on a certain Great Adventure.

Perhaps her womanly intuition sensed danger, for Carly joined with Peter's sister in her entreaties that he spend his vacation nearer home.

"But I don't want to," stated Peter, with the air of one giving a full explanation.

"That settles it," sighed Julie; "what Peter Boots wants is law in this house."

"Autocrat! Tyrant! Oppressor!" and Carlotta wrinkled her little nose in an effort to express scornful disdain.

"Yes," Peter agreed, with his benignant smile, "despot, demagogue, dictator, oligarch, lord of the roost and cock of the walk! It's a great thing to be monarch of all one surveys!"

"To the surveyor," flouted Carlotta, "but if you knew what the surveyed think of you!"

"I'd be all puffed up with pride and vanity, I suppose," Peter nodded his still golden head, though Time's caressing fingers had burnished the yellow to a deeper bronze.

"You'll break mother's heart," suggested Julie, but in a hopelessly resigned tone.

"Only the same old break, sister, and it's been cracked and mended so many times, I'm sure it'll stand another smash."

"Oh, he's going, and that's all there is about it," said Carlotta with the air of a fatalist.

"I'm going," Peter assented, "but that isn't all there is about it. I'm coming back!" and he looked at the girl with unmistakable intent.

"Maybe and maybe not," she returned, with crushing carelessness, whether real or assumed.

"Yes, indeed, maybe and maybe not!" put in Julie. "You don't know about the prophecy, Carly! Shall I tell her, Peter?"

"Tell me, of course," and Miss Harper looked eagerly interested. "Who prophesied what? and when?"

"Oh, it was years ago," Julie began, "we met a lot of gypsies, and mother would have them tell the family fortunes. And one of them said that Peter would go off on a long journey and that he would die a terrible death and never come home."

"Oh," Carly shuddered, "don't tell me any more!"

"But the more is the best part of it," said Peter, smiling; "you see, mother was so upset by this direful news, that another gypsy took pity on her and amended my cruel fate. The second seeress declared that I must meet the destiny number one had dealt me, but that to mitigate the family grief, I would return afterwards."

"As a spook?" cried Carlotta, "how interesting!"

"Perhaps; but it doesn't interest me at present You see, this trip is not the fatal one——"

"How do you know?" from Julie.

"Oh, it's too soon. That old prophecy isn't fairly ripe yet. Moreover, I'm not ready for it. I'm going to Labrador,—and I'm coming back,—and then, if all goes well, perhaps I'll never want to go away again. And if not,——" he looked at Carly, "I may be glad to take the last and final trip! But if I go on with the program and return as my own ghost, I'll lead you girls a dance! I'll haunt you in season and out of season!"

"Pooh, I'm not afraid," Carly tossed her head; "I've no faith in any of this spiritist foolery."

"Don't call it foolery, my child," said a serious voice, as Peter's father came into the room.

Benjamin Crane gave the impression of power and gentleness, a fine combination and rarely seen in its perfection. A man of sixty, he looked older, for his thick hair was white and his smoothly shaven face was lined with deep furrows.

He joined the group of young people, and it was indicative of his nature that there was no pause in the conversation or appearance of constraint of any sort.

"But it is foolery, Mr. Crane," Carlotta defended, "I've tried the Ouija Board myself, and it's a silly business."

"Not so silly as to condemn something you know little or nothing about," Mr. Crane said, in his serious, kindly way. "My dear Carlotta, even though you don't 'believe in' the supernatural, do try to realize that your lack of belief doesn't bar the rest of us from having faith in revelation."

"Oh, that's all right, Mr. Crane," Carly wasn't a bit offended, "don't mind me! Believe all you want to. But, do you believe in this 'Gypsy's Warning' about Peter? That's different, you know, from the usual claptrap."

"It's not exactly a question of belief," Mr. Crane said, slowly. "You will, I am sure, agree that Peter may be killed on some of these wild and dangerous adventures in which his soul delights. Let us hope the day is far off, if it must come at all. And as to his spirit's return,—that is, of course, possible,—to my mind, at least."

"If possible, then extremely probable," declared Peter, laughing; "I've just told the girls, Dad, that I'll haunt them like a continuous performance, if conditions allow. Want me to appear to you, too?"

"Don't be so flippant, Son. If you die while away from us, and if your spirit can return and communicate with me, I shall, indeed, be glad to receive such messages, no matter through what medium."

"Oh, goodness, gracious!" exclaimed Carlotta; "not through a medium, I beg of you, Peter! I don't want spook messages that way! I don't mind a nice little Ouija or Planchette, but a common, blowsy, untidy medium person,—and they're all like that,—I can't stand for!"

"Why, you little rascal, what do *you* know about mediums?" Peter Boots frowned at her.

"I went to a *seance* once,—but, wow! never again!"

"I should hope not! You stay away from such places, or I won't come home to you at all,—dead or alive! How would you like that?"

"Not at all, oh, despot, oligarch, Grand Panjandrum,— or whatever you call yourself. Please come back, and all will be forgiven."

It was tea time in the Crane home, and though the home was only a summer cottage, up Westchester way, yet the big living room, with its hospitable easy chairs and occasional tables, its willow and chintz, gave an impression of an English household. It was late in July and, though warm, it was not sultry, and the breeze coming in at the big windows was crisp and fresh.

Mrs. Crane drifted into the room almost at the same moment two men appeared from outdoors.

A happy complacency was the chief attribute of Peter's mother, and this spoke from every smile of her amiable face and every movement of her plump but still graceful form.

As Peter adjusted the cushions she took a low willow chair and smiled a greeting at all, including the newcomers.

These were Kit Shelby and Gilbert Blair, the two companions of the Labrador trip.

They were good-looking, well set-up chaps, quite evidently unable to talk of anything save the plans for the momentous journey.

"Got a wonder for a guide," began Shelby, as soon as decent greetings had been made. "He's just been let loose by Sir Somebody of Somewhere, and I nailed him. Name o' Joshua,—but we can stand that. He really knows it all,—without continually proclaiming the fact."

"I'm thankful that you've a fine guide," murmured Mrs. Crane, in her satisfied way. "It means so much to me to know that."

"You're right, Lady Crane," assented young Blair. "And old Peter will have to obey him, too."

"Of course I shall," put in Peter. "I always bow to authority, when it's greater than my own. Oh, won't it all be great! I'm crazy to start. Think of it, Dad,—we three fellows sitting around a camp fire, smoking our pipes and spinning yarns of an evening, after a long day's hike over the ice and snow!"

"Thought you were going in a canoe," said his sister.

"Part of the way,—but, later, we abandon the craft and hoof it."

"Maybe and maybe not," said Shelby. "It all depends on the weather conditions. But the season is just right, and we'll have good going, one way or another, I'm sure."

"You're the surest thing I know, Kit," Gilbert Blair said; "now with no hint of pessimism, I own up I look for pretty hard lines a good bit of the time."

"Calamity Howler!" returned Shelby; "why damp our enthusiasm like that?"

"Can't damp mine," and Peter beamed with glad anticipation. "Let the hard lines come if they like. I'm expecting them and expecting to enjoy them along with the rest."

"Pollyanna Peter!" chaffed Carlotta; "shan't you mind it if the blizzard blows down your tent and the dogs run away with your dinner and your feets give out?"

"Nixy! I'll set up the tent again, get some more dinner from the larder and rest my feet for a spell."

"That's right, boy," said his father, "that's the spirit. But do take enough provisions and, if they run low, make a dash for home."

"Just my idea, Dad, exactly. And as Shelby's looking after the commissariat, and Blair attending to the tents and cooking outfit, something tells me they'll be top hole. Maybe not such traps as these——" and Peter nodded toward the elaborate tea service being brought in and arranged before Mrs. Crane, who was in her element as hostess.

"No, you poor boys," she said, "I suppose you'll drink out of horrible thick china——"

"Not china at all, ma'am," corrected Blair; "lovely white enamel, though, with blue edges——"

"I know!" cried Carlotta, "like our motor lunch-box."

"Yes, that sort, and not bad, either. Oh, we'll rough it more or less, but it won't be absolutely primitive,—not by a long shot!"

"It'll be absolutely perfect," said Peter, dreamily gazing off into space, and seeing in his mind great white stretches of snowy landscape, or black, gurgling holes in ice-bound rivers.

"You are so ridiculous!" declared his sister. "You're a regular Sybarite at home. You love easy chairs and pillows and fresh flowers all about, and all that,—then you want to go off where you'll have nothing nice at all,— not even a laundry!"

"Right you are, Sis. The Human warious is hard to understand. Come along, Carly, take me for a walk."

Rather slowly the girl rose, and the two sauntered forth, across the wide veranda, across the lawn and down a garden path. Neither spoke until, coming to a marble bench, they sat down and turned to look into each other's eyes.

"Going to say yes before I go, Carly, or after I come back?"

"After you come back," was the prompt response.

"Oh, good! You promise to say it *then*?"

"Well, I don't say how *soon* after."

"I'll decide on the soonness. Then I take it we're engaged?"

"You take it nothing of the sort! You know, Peter Crane, you can't boss me as you do your own family!"

"Heaven forbid! Why, dear, I want you to boss me! Our life together will be one grand boss,—and you can be it!"

"Don't be silly, I'm in earnest. I couldn't be happy with a dominating, domineering man."

"Of course you couldn't. But I assure you I'm not one. You see, I only dictate in my own family because they like to have me to do so. Mother would be awfully upset if I didn't tell her what to do. Dad the same,—although I'm not sure the old dear knows it himself. And as for Julie,— why she just depends on me. So I naturally gravitate to the place of Grand Mogul, because I can't help it. But with you, it's different. You're a whole heap wiser, better and more fit to rule than I. And if you'll rule me, I'll be greatly obliged,—honest, I will."

"Oh, you're so absurd, Peter! I don't want to rule, either. I want us to be equally interested in everything, and have equal say in any matter."

"All right,—equality goes. I'll race you to see which can be the equalest. Now, are we engaged?"

"No, Peter, not till you come back."

"But I want to kiss you, and I can't, I suppose, until we are engaged. Oh, can I?"

"Of course not! Take your hand off my hand."

"Lordy, can't I even touch your hand?"

"Not with that ownership grasp! I am afraid of your possessive qualities, Peter."

"Meaning just what?"

"Oh, that if I do give myself to you, you'll own me so— so emphatically."

"I sure shall! And then some. Don't imagine, my child, that I'll accept you with any reservations. You'll be 'mine to the core of your heart, my beauty'! Bank on that!"

"I do,—and if I'm yours at all,—it *will* be that way. But wait till you come back. There's time enough. I suppose there's no chance for letters?"

"No; not after the first few days. We'll be out of reach of mail very soon."

"And you're returning?"

"I want to be home for Christmas. Kit thinks we'll make it, but Blair is some doubtful. So, look for me when you see me."

"Alive or dead?"

"Carly! What made you say that?"

"I don't know." The girl shuddered and her eyes stared into Peter's. "I seemed to say it without any volition,—the words just came——"

"Well, don't let them come again. I don't like it a little bit. I'm coming home alive, very much alive,—and I'm coming home to claim you,—remember that."

"Unless either of us falls in love with some one else. Those girls of the far North are beautiful, I hear."

"An Eskimo with a nose ring? No, thank you! My heart is true to Poll! But don't you go and set your somewhat fickle heart on another man, 'cause if you do, I shall have to kill him, much as I'd regret such a necessity."

"My heart isn't fickle! What do you mean?"

"Just what I say. I think it is. I think my little black-eyed, rosy-cheeked Carly is quite capable of being on with a new love whether she's off with the old or not."

"Oh, Peter," and the black eyes showed moisture, "how cruel you are!"

"Isn't it so, Carly? Tell me it isn't,—I'll be so glad!"

But the coquettish glance that answered him was not entirely reassuring.

"Anyway," Peter pleaded on, "tell me you like me better than Kit or Gilbert. Tell me that if I'm a prey to green-eyed jealousy up there in the camp, at least, I needn't envy either of those chaps."

"Of course not!"

"Oh, you torment! Your words are all right,—but your emphasis is a little too strong. Carly, look me straight in the eyes and tell me you don't care for either of them!"

"Either of your eyes?"

"Silly! Well, yes, then, tell me that!"

The chicory flower eyes looked into the great, dark ones, and for a moment there was silence. The blue eyes were sweet and true, and they burned with a strong, deep lovelight. The eyes that gazed into them fell a little and seemed unable to meet them squarely.

"What is it, Carly? What is it, dear?" he begged.

"Nothing," she said, lightly. "I do l-like you, Peter,— better than any man I know——"

"Better than Kit Shelby?"

"Yes."

"Better than Gil Blair?"

"Yes."

"They're the ones I most feared. And mostly because I didn't want to go on a trip with a man I'm jealous of! That would be a fine kettle of fish!"

"Well, you won't do that. Don't worry about them,—or any one else."

"Oh, you blessed little girl! Carly, dearest, why can't you say yes, now? Won't you, Carly,—please."

The caressing voice was low and gentle, the pleading blue eyes were very earnest, but Carlotta still shook her head.

"When you come back," she repeated.

"All right, then," and Peter's face showed one of its masterful looks. "I'll accept your decree,—as I can't very well help myself, but just as sure as you're sitting there, Carly Harper, I'm going to kiss you!"

And he did; gathering her into his arms with a gentle insistence and kissing her squarely on her surprised red lips.

"There!" he said, "I guess you'll remember now that you belong to me,—whether you call yourself engaged or not! Mad?"

"Yes," she responded, but the one swift glance she gave him belied her words.

"You'll get over it," he said, cheerfully. "I'd like to kiss you again, though. May I?"

"When you come back," she said, and Peter waited.

CHAPTER 2: THE LABRADOR WILD

It was late in July before Peter Boots marshaled his merry men and let himself be marshaled by the guide, Joshua, on the trip of exploration and recreation.

A liner took them as far as Newfoundland, and at St. John's, a smaller steamer, the *Victoria Lake*, received them for their journey farther North. This ship belonged to a sealing fleet and also carried mails. It was not especially comfortable, and neither staterooms nor food were of the best.

But Peter was discomfort-proof, and his negligence of bothersome details and happy acceptance of existing conditions set a standard for the manners and customs of their party. Joshua, who had come to New York City to meet them, was not, by nature, possessed of the sort of heart that doeth good like medicine. But under the sunny smile of Peter's blue eyes, his customary scowl softened to a look of mild wonder at the effervescent gayety of the man who was yet so efficient and even hard-working when occasion required it.

Shelby was a close second in the matter of efficiency. He was a big chap, not handsome, but good-looking, in a dark, dignified way, and of a lithe, sinewy strength that enabled him to endure as well as to meet hardship bravely.

Not that they looked especially for hardships. Discomfort, even unpleasantness, they did anticipate, but nothing of more importance than inclement weather or possible colds or coughs. And against the latter ills Mrs. Crane had provided both remedies and preventions to such an extent that some were discarded as excess weight.

For the necessities of their trip, including as they did, canoe, tent, blankets, tarpaulins, duffel bags, shooting irons and cooking utensils,—besides food, were of no small bulk and weight even divided among four porters.

And Blair, though possessed of will and energy quite equaling the others', was less physically fit to stand the hard going.

It was already August when they were treated to a first sight of the Labrador.

"Great Scott!" exclaimed Shelby, "and Shackelton, and Peary,—yes and old Doc Cook! What an outlook! If those breaking waves were looking for a stern and rockbound coast to dash on, they missed it when they chose the New England shore instead of this! I've seen crags and cliffs, I've climbed the dark brow of the mighty Helvellyn, but this puts it over all the earth! How do we get in, anyway?"

"Great, isn't it?" and Peter lay back in his inadequate little deck chair and beamed at the desolation he saw.

For the coast of Labrador is nearly a thousand miles of barren bleakness and forbidding and foreboding rock wall. After buffeting untold ages of icy gales and biting storms the bare rocks seem to discourage human approach and crave only their own black solitude.

The one softening element was the fog that rode the sea, and now and then swooped down, hiding the dangerous reefs until the danger was increased tenfold by the obscurity.

"Oh, great!" mocked Shelby. "You can have mine. I'm going to stay on the boat and go back."

"Yes, you are!" grinned Peter, knowing full well how little importance to attach to that speech; "inside of a week, you'll be crazy about it."

"I am now," said Blair, slowly. "Most weird sight I ever saw. The rocks seem like sentient giants ready to eat each other. Termagant Nature, unleashed and rampant."

"Idea all right," said Crane, lazily, "but your verbiage isn't hand-picked, seems to me."

"You can put it more poetically, if you like, but it's the thing itself that gets me, not the sand-papered description of it."

"Nobody wants you to sand-paper it, but you ought to hew to the line a little more nearly——"

"Lines be bothered! Free verse is the thing for this place!"

"I want free verse and I want fresh air," bantered Peter, "and Lasca, down by the Brandywine,—or wherever it was that Friend Lasca hung out."

"You're harking back to your school days and Friday afternoon declamation," put in Shelby, "and Lasca was down by the Rio Grande."

"Only Alaska isn't down there at all," Blair informed them, quite seriously, and the others roared.

*   *   *   *   *

After delays, changes and transfers made necessary by the uncertainties of Labrador travel, they came at last to Hamilton Inlet, and the little steamer approached the trading post at Rigolet.

"Reminds me of Hamilton Harbor, Bermuda," observed Shelby, shivering as he drew his furs round him.

"Oh, how can you!" exclaimed Blair; "that heavenly Paradise of a place,—and this!"

"But you'd rather be here?" and Crane shook a warning fist at him.

"Yes,—oh, yes! This is the life!" and if Blair wasn't quite sincere he gave a fair imitation of telling the truth.

"Will you look at the dogs!" cried Crane. "I didn't know there were so many in the world!"

The big Eskimo dogs were prowling about, growling a little, and appearing anything but friendly. Not even to sunny-faced and kindly-voiced Peter Boots did they respond, but snarled and pawed the ground until Joshua advised Crane to let them alone.

"They're mighty good things to keep away from," the guide informed, and his advice was taken.

"I'm glad we have a trusty canoe instead of those villainous looking creatures," Blair admitted, and when, later on, they heard tales of the brutality and treachery of the pack dogs, the others agreed.

At Rigolet final arrangements were decided on and last purchases made for the dash into the wilds.

Peter Boots, in his element, was as excited and pleased as a child with a new toy.

"Here I am, where I've longed to be!" he exulted; "at least, I'm on my way. Buck up, you fellows, and enjoy yourselves, or you'll answer to me why not!"

"I'm for it," Kit Shelby cried; "I hated that dinky little old steamer, but now we're ashore in this live wire of a place, I'm as excited and glad as anybody. I say, the mail from England comes every year! Think of that!"

"Once a year!" wondered Blair.

"Yep; the good ship *Pelican* brought it yesterday, and it's due again next summer! Up and coming, this place, I tell you!"

"It nothing means to us," said Crane, calmly; "I'm expecting no valentines from England myself, and we'll be back home before mails from the States get around again."

"And, moreover," said Shelby, who had been acquiring information by various means, "old Captain Whiskers, forninst, says that we're bound to get lost, strayed and stolen if we go the route we've planned."

"That's our route, then!" Peter said, satisfiedly; "they always prophesy all sorts of dismal fates, and, like dreams, they go by contraries. 'Fraid, boys!"

He extricated himself from the onslaught this speech brought and then all set about getting the outfit into shape for the start.

Pounds and pounds of flour, bacon, lard, pea meal, tea, coffee, rice, tobacco and other necessaries were packed and stowed and maneuvered by the capable

Joshua, before whose superior judgment Peter Boots had to bow.

Some natives were hired to help carry things that were to be cached against the return trip, and three tired but happy men went to rest for their last night beneath a real roof for many weeks.

Next morning their happiness was even greater and their spirits higher, for the day was clear and perfect, the air full of exhilarating ozone and the golden sunlight and deep blue sky seemed to promise a fair trip and a safe return.

Gayly they started off, and gayly they continued, save when the rain poured unpleasantly, or the swarms of Labrador flies attacked them or steep banks or swift rapids made portage difficult.

However as no threats or persuasions could induce Joshua to travel in the rain, there were enforced rests that helped in the long run.

Another trial was the midday heat. Though the temperature might be at the freezing point at night, by noon it would buoyantly rise to ninety degrees, and the sudden changes made for colds and coughs, that were not easily cured by Mrs. Crane's nostrums.

"Fortunes of war," said Peter, serenely, and Shelby responded, "If that's what they are, I'm a regular profiteer!"

Days went by, the hours filled with alternate joy and woe, but accepted philosophically by willing hearts who had already learned to love the vicissitudes of the wild.

One morning a portage route was of necessity winding and rough. Not as much as usual could be carried by any of them and two or three trips of two miles must be made by each.

Joshua arranged the loads to weigh about seventy pounds each, but these became tiresome after a time. The work took all day, and when toward sunset camp was made and the tired pleasure seekers sought rest, each was far more exhausted than he was willing to admit.

"Had enough?" asked Peter, smiling. "Turn back any time you fellows say. Want to quit?"

"Quit! Never!" declared Shelby. "Go home when you like, or stay as long as you please, but no quitting!"

"It's goin' be nice now," put in Joshua, who was always sensitive to any discontent with his beloved North land. "Nice fishin', nice sleepin',—oh, yes!"

And there was. Rest that night on couches of spruce branches, that rocked like a cradle, and smelled like Araby the Blest, more than knit up the raveled sleeve of the hard day before.

And when they fished in a small, rocky stream, for heaven sent trout, contentment could go no further. Unless it might have been when later they ate the same trout, cooked to a turn by the resourceful Joshua, and then, lounging at ease before a camp-fire that met all traditions, they smoked and talked or were silent as the spirit moved.

The black firs showed gaunt against the sky; the stars came out in twinkling myriads and the dash and roar of the river was an accompaniment to their desultory chat.

"If I were a poet," Blair said, "I'd quote poetry about now."

"Your own, for choice?" asked Shelby, casually.

"You *are* a poet, Gil," said Peter. "I've noticed it all the way along. You don't have to lisp in numbers to be a poet. You just have to——"

"Well, to what?" asked Blair, as Peter paused.

"Why, you just have to want to recite poetry."

"Yes, that's it," put in Shelby, quickly; "understand, Gilbert, dear, you don't have to recite it, you know, only want to recite it. If you obey your impulse,—you're no poet at all."

"I'll restrain the impulse then,—but it's hard—hard!"

"Oh, go ahead," laughed Kit, "if it's as hard as all that! I'll bet it's highbrow stuff you want to get out of your system!"

"Yes, it is. In fact it's Browning."

"Oh, I don't mind him. Fire away."

"Only this bit:

"You're my friend;
What a thing friendship is, world without end.
How it gives the heart and the senses a stir-up,
As if somebody broached you a glorious runlet——"

"That'll do," laughed Peter. "That's far enough. And you didn't say it quite right, any way."

"No matter," said Blair, earnestly; "I mean the thing. Without any palaver, we three fellows are friends,—and I'm glad of it. That's all."

"Thank you very much," said Shelby, "for my share. And old Pete is fairly overflowing with appreciation,—I see it in his baby-blue eyes——"

"I'll baby you!" said Peter, with a ferocious smile. "Yes, old Gilbert, we're friends, or I shouldn't have picked us as the fittest for this trip."

"Good you did, for the fittest have the reputation of surviving."

"Let up on the croaks," Peter spoke abruptly. "Have you noticed any fearful dangers, that you apprehend non-survival of them?"

"No; but——"

"But nothing! Now, Blairsy, if you're in thoughtful mood, let's go on with that plot we started yesterday."

"What plot?' asked Shelby.

"Oh, a great motive for a story or play. Setting up here in the Labrador wilds and——"

Shelby yawned. "Mind if I doze off?" he said; "this fire is soporific——"

"Don't mind a bit," returned Peter gayly; "rather you would, then Gil and I can maudle on as we like."

And they did. Both were of a literary turn, and though they had achieved nothing of importance as yet, both hoped to write sooner or later.

"A story," Peter said, "maybe a book, but more likely a short story, with a real O. Henry punch."

"H'mph!" came in a disdainful grunt from the dozing Shelby.

"You keep still, old lowbrow," advised Peter. "Don't sniff at your betters. There's a great little old plot here, and we're going to make a good thing of it and push it along."

"Push away," and Shelby rolled himself over and dozed again.

"Where's Joshua?" asked Crane, later, as, the talk over, they prepared to bunk on their evergreen boughs.

"Haven't seen him since supper," said Shelby, sitting up and rubbing his eyes. "Queer, isn't it?"

Queer it surely was, and more so, as time went by and they could find no trace of their guide.

"He can't be lost," said Kit; "he's too good a scout for that."

"He can't have deserted us," declared Peter. "He's too good a friend for that! He'll no more desert us than we'd desert one another."

"Well, he's missing anyway," Blair said, undeniably; "then something must have happened. Could he be caught in a trap?"

"Not he! he's used to them about. No, he's had an accident, I think." Peter's eyes were anxious and his voice told of a fear of some real disaster.

The dusk fell early and though only about nine o'clock, it was as dark as midnight. Clouds had obscured the stars, and only the firelight relieved the black darkness.

But after an hour's worriment and distress on the part of the three men the guide returned. He looked a little shame-faced, and was disinclined to reply to their questions.

"Come, now, Joshua, own up," directed Peter; "I see by your eyes you've been up to mischief. Out with it!"

"I—I got lost!" was the astonishing reply, and they all burst into laughter. More at the rueful countenance, however, than at the news, for it was a serious matter.

"You, a guide, lost!" exclaimed Shelby. "How did it happen?"

"Dunno. Jest somehow couldn't find the way."

"Hadn't you a compass?"

"No, sir; I got sort of turned around like,—and I went a long hike the wrong way."

Simply enough, to be sure, but apparently it was only good fortune that had made him find at last the road home to camp.

Light-hearted Peter dismissed the whole affair with a "Look out after this; and always carry a compass or take one of us boys along," and then he sought his fragrant, if not altogether downy couch.

Blair, too, gave the episode little thought, but to Shelby it seemed more important. If a hardened guide could get lost as easily as that, it might happen to any of them. And a compass was not a sure safeguard. A man could wander round and round without finding a fairly nearby camp. Shelby was a few years older than the other two, and of a far more prudent nature. He had no dare-devil instincts, and not an overweening love of adventure. He was enjoying his trip because of the outdoor life and wildwood sports, but as for real adventure, he was content to omit it. Not from fear—Kit Shelby was as brave as any,—but he saw no sense in taking unnecessary risks.

While risks were as the breath of life to Peter Boots. Indeed, he was sighing because the conditions of modern camping ways and the efficiency of the guide left little or no chance for risk of life or limb.

He didn't by any means want to lose life or limb, but he was not at all unwilling to risk them pretty desperately. And he found no opportunity. The days were pleasantly taken up with fishing, shooting, moving on, setting up and taking down camp, and all the expected routine of a mountain expedition; but, so far, there had been nothing unusual or even uncomfortable to any great degree.

The next day brought a fearful storm, with gales and sleet and driving rain and the temperature dropped many degrees.

The party experienced their first really cold weather, and though it depressed the others Peter seemed to revel in it.

The tent was practically a prison, and an uncomfortable one, for the wind was terrific and the squalls became hourly more menacing.

Shelby was quiet, by reason of a sore throat, and Blair was quiet with a silence that was almost sulky.

Not quite though, for irrepressible Peter kept the crowd good-natured, by the simple process of making jokes and laughing at them himself, so contagiously, that all were forced to join in.

But at last he tired of that, and announced that he was going to write letters.

"Do," said Shelby, "and hurry up with them. The postman will be along any minute now."

Peter grinned, and really set himself to work with paper and pencil.

"I know what you're doing," said Blair; "you're beginning our story."

"I'm not, but that isn't half a bad idea. Let's start in, Gil. We can plan it and make up names and things——"

"Why can't you really write it?" asked Shelby. "I should think it would be the psychological moment. Isn't it to be all about the storms and other indigenous delights of Labrador?"

"You take that tone and I'll pitch you out into the indigenous delights," threatened Peter. "Come on, Gilbert, let's block out the backbone of the yarn right now."

They set to work, and by dint of much discussing, disagreeing, ballyragging and bulldozing each other, they did make a fair start.

"What's the heroine like?" asked Shelby, beginning to be interested.

"Like Carly Harper," said Blair promptly.

"Not the leastest, littlest mite like Carly Harper," said Peter, his blue eyes hardening with determination.

"Why not?" demanded Blair, who cared little what the heroine was like; but who objected to contradiction without reason.

"Because I say not," returned Peter, impatiently. "The heroine is a little rosy-cheeked, flaxen-haired doll. She has blue eyes,—something like mine,—and a saucy, turn-up nose, and a dimple in her left cheek."

"A peach," said Shelby, "but no sort of a heroine for that yarn you two fellows are spinning. I'm no author, but I'm an architect, and I can see the incongruity."

"If you know so much, write it yourself," said Peter, but not pettishly. "If I'm doing it, I create my own heroine or I quit."

"Oh, don't quit," begged Blair. "We're just getting a good start. Have the treacle and taffy heroine if you like, only keep on."

His point won, Peter did keep on, and a fair bit of work was accomplished. For the first time it began to seem as if the two authors would really produce something worth while.

"Not likely," Peter said, as they talked this over. "I'm no sort of a collaborator,—I'm too set in my ways. If I can't have it the way I want it, I can't do it at all."

"But you can have your own way in details," said Blair, musingly. "They don't matter much. Give me the swing of the plot and let me plan the climaxes, and I care not who makes the laws for the heroine's complexion."

"Well, I'm for a run in the rain," said Peter. "I've worked my brain into a tangled snarl, and I must go out and clear it out."

He shook himself into his storm togs, and as no one cared to go with him, he started off alone.

CHAPTER 3: THE SNOWSTORM

Given three good-natured young men, a satisfactory guide, a stretch of Labrador wild, and no cares of any sort, it is not surprising that the happy days and weeks followed one another into the maw of Time, until the date of departure for home drew near.

"I'd like to stay here forever," declared Blair, as he filled his pipe and stretched luxuriously before the fire. "Civilization has lost all charm for me."

"Go away with you!" scoffed Peter Boots, "that's a fine, ambitious spirit to show, and you a rising young author,—or about to become one."

"Not unless you duff in and help, old chap. Our book hangs on your efforts, I've pretty well done my part of it."

"And I'll do mine, don't worry. I'm a procrastinator and a put-offer, but I'll get there! Now, cut out the book till we get home. These last few days up here must be given over to Nature as she is snowed under!"

It was the last week in September, but snow-squalls were frequent, winds were high and rains were cold and sleety.

Joshua had been urging the homeward journey for several days, but the men were loath to go, until now, a more severe bit of weather had persuaded them. Even as they sat round the fire, with storm coats drawn high up around their ears, the sleet-squalls drove against their faces and the gale howled among the snowy trees.

Peter loved the life, the outdoor days and tented nights, but his mind once made up to leave, his volatile spirit turned toward home.

"A couple of days more staving round in the snowdrifts and I'll be ready," he announced, and Joshua began to pack up.

The guide growled a little at the reluctance of his party to start.

"You men wait too long, and you'll be sorry," he warned. "This wind won't only let up for a little spell at a time,—mostly it'll blow like somethin' let loose! And if a big snow comes,—and it's likely to,—we'll be in a fix."

"Now, now, old man," began Shelby, "don't growl. We've been a pretty good sort, haven't we? We're going home, aren't we? Why croak at us?"

"That's all right, sir, but meantime this Northwest wind keeps up its force, and—well, it means business."

"All right, we'll get the better of its business deal," prophesied Peter, and he and Blair went off for a hike.

As they started, the sun shone clear, and though the temperature was below thirty, the two men strode along, happy with sheer physical joy of living.

"This is the life!" said Peter, flapping his arms, and watching his breath congeal in frosty clouds.

"Yes," Blair agreed, "to a certain point——"

"Freezing point?"

"I guess that's right! I like it all as well as you do, but it's nicest when the sun shines. And by Jiminy, she's clouding over again!"

Clouds meant cold,—a raw, penetrating chill that seemed to strike to the marrow, and the pair were glad to turn back toward camp.

"What do you think most about, when you think of home?" asked Blair, idly.

"Carly Harper," replied Peter, speaking from the fullness of his heart.

"Good Lord! So do I!" exclaimed Blair, his tone that of surprise only.

Peter turned and looked at him. "Not a chance for you, old chap," he said. "Little Carly is waiting for me. Yeo, ho, lads, ho,—Yeo, ho!"

"Oh, I say! Really?" Blair's consternation was almost comic.

"Yes, sir! Fair warning,—keep off!"

"Engaged?"

"Same as."

"Meaning she hasn't said a positive yes?"

"Meaning that, if you like."

"Then it's fair field and no favor! We're too good friends to misunderstand, but let's call it a case of may the best man win."

"All right, but I'll win and you can be best man at the wedding, how's that?" Peter's eyes shone with good humor, and his happy face left Blair little room for doubt as to Peter's own view of the case. What Carly herself thought was another matter.

But the two were too good friends to quarrel, and moreover, each knew the other too well to mistrust him for a minute. It would, indeed, be a fair field where they were concerned.

"I didn't know you'd gone so far," said Blair, ruefully, "of course, there's no chance for me."

"I hope not," returned Peter, cheerfully. "But when we get back we'll soon find out."

"Perhaps find out that she's 'gone with a handsomer man,'" suggested Blair.

"Not impossible. I suppose there are such."

But a disinterested observer, looking at Peter's fine, strong face, with its radiant coloring, brought out by the sharp air, might not have agreed.

And then conversation became abstract, for the wind rose to a piercing gale and it was all they could do to keep their balance and fight their way along.

* * * * *

"I said this here wind was bound to ease up some time and it has," said Joshua, with decided satisfaction, the morning of the start for home. "We ought to make good goin' to-day, and maybe get ahead of our own schedule."

"That's the trick," said Shelby, "always get ahead of your own schedule, and you're bound to succeed. Come on, Peter, here we go."

The leave-taking was a bit silent, for all three had become attached to the camp, and they gave long farewell glances backward.

Then off they went, and throwing sentiment aside, turned their thoughts and their talk to the coming journey.

For home was yet a long way off. Many days' traveling before they reached the mail boat and then many more before they could lift New York Harbor.

"And I'm glad of it," declared Peter. "The longer we are on the home stretch, the better I'll be pleased."

"Granting we don't miss the boat," added Blair. "When I start out I want to arrive."

It was about three days later that a big storm set in. Relentlessly it blew and snowed and the gales were almost unbreastable.

"Don't dare stop," said Joshua, in his usual laconic way; "the winter's set in, and any day may be worse'n the day before. Old Merk is down to twenty-four, and we want to peg ahead,—that's what we want to do."

They did,—by day,—and by night they enjoyed the rest and warmth of camp, but still, Joshua urged them ahead continually.

He parceled out longer days and shorter nights, until even strong Peter began to feel the strain.

Shelby was of a wiry sort, and stood hard going well; Blair was a patient, plodding nature and wouldn't have complained if he had dropped in his tracks; but Peter was impulsive and impatient, and he growled frankly.

"We'll get there, Eli," he said to the guide; "don't hustle us so."

"Got to do it, Mr. Crane. I know more about this here winter that's closing in on us, than you do. It's a bit early, but it's sure!"

So on they went, through snow that was wet and heavy, through icy sleet that stung and cut their faces, through roaring winds that choked their lungs, but full of indomitable courage and perseverance and of unimpaired good nature.

And yet a week of this traveling at last began to tell on their *morale*. Not that they grew testy or irritable, but the silences were longer, the repartee less gay, and even buoyant Peter's spirits drooped a little.

Joshua then took a turn as comforter.

"The worst'll soon be over," he reassured them. "Two days will get us to Big Lake, and once we finish that, we'll be well on our way."

So on they pushed, heavily laden, traveling slowly, but all well and sound in wind and limb.

It was the middle of October, when a bright sunny day beamed on them and their spirits rose in consequence.

But Joshua did not smile. "Weather breeder," he said, laconically, and looked gloomy.

The others knew better than to call him a pessimist, for when Joshua predicted weather, it came.

And come it did. Not a squall; there was little if any wind, but a snowfall. A steady, straight down snow that was so thick, so dense, they could scarce see one another's forms.

"Keep a-going," directed Joshua; "and for the land's sake, don't get far apart. Stay close together, single trail, and close!"

Thus they went on, the guide first, then Shelby, then Blair, then Peter. There was no reason for the order they took, it merely happened that it was so.

They kept close, as directed, but the going was hard. If one stumbled, one must recover quickly and hasten ahead not to lose sight of the others.

And the snow continued. Soft, white, feathery flakes, more and more thickly falling every moment. Joshua plowed ahead, the others followed, and each had all he could do to keep his eyes clear enough to see the man in front.

Which is how it happened that when Peter stumbled and fell, and found himself unable to rise, the others had no knowledge of it.

As the big man went down, he essayed to rise quickly, but his right leg refused to move.

"Broken!" he said to himself, as one noting a trivial occurrence. "Queer, to break a leg, falling in a bed of soft snow!"

But that was exactly what he had done, and realizing it, he set up a yell that would have made a North American Indian envy its force and volume.

But for all the good it did, it might as well have been a whisper. The wind, though not violent, was against him, and carried the sound away from the plodding travelers. His friends could not hear it. Not looking back, as indeed, they had no thought of doing, they did not miss their fallen comrade and on they toiled, ignorant of the fact that they were three instead of four now.

And Peter,—big, strong Peter Crane,—brave, intrepid Peter Boots,—sat there in the furious snowstorm, unable to rise, but with brain and mind vividly alive to what had happened.

Quick of thought, always, he now traced with lightning rapidity, just what the future held for him—and such a short future, at that—unless——

His only hope lay in his lung power.

He yelled, screamed, whistled, hooted, and put all of his strength and nerve force in his desperate efforts to reach the ears of his comrades.

But it was impossible. The cruel wind drove his voice away from those it was meant to reach, the snowflakes filled his open mouth as he shouted; and as hope failed, strength failed and Peter faced his fate.

Strong, able-bodied, save for the broken leg, he tried to crawl along. The result was pitiful, for he merely floundered in the deep mass of soft whiteness. His share of the luggage was heavy packs, nothing of which he could make a flag of distress or even build a fire. He felt for his matches, and lighting a cigarette, waved it aloft, almost smiling at his tiny beacon. Then came despair. His mind seemed to grow more alert as his body was overcome by the cold. His blood boiled, even as it froze in his veins. He felt abnormally acute of intellect, and plead with himself to think of something,—to invent something that would save his life.

Yet he knew there was no hope. The fast-falling snow obliterated all tracks almost instantly. Even though the others missed him, they could never find him, and,—this thought struck a new chill through his veins,—in a short time the snowfall would even obliterate him!

What a death! Helpless; unable even to meet it standing, he must lie there, and let the snow bury him alive!

He could maintain a half-sitting posture,—but what use? Why not lie down flat and get it over quickly? Yet he must hold on as long as possible, for the men might come back,—he began to think what they would do—but, he was sure they would not miss him until too late to do anything. If the snow would only let up. It was such a pity to have his whereabouts hidden by a foolish fall of snow! As Peter grew colder he grew calmer. His senses mercifully became numbed at last, and as the actual moment of his freezing to death came nearer and nearer, he cared less and less. A state of coma is a blessing to many dying men, and into this state Peter gently drifted, even as the snow drifted over and covered his stiff, silent form.

* * * * *

And his friends trudged on; not that it could be called trudging,—rather, they plodded, stumbled, pitched, fought and merely achieved progress by blindly plunging ahead.

It was nearly a half hour after Peter's fall that Blair, accidentally turned round by a gust of wind, called out an exasperated "Halloo!" which gained no response.

"Halloo!" he repeated, "Peter! how goes it?"

Still no return call, and Blair called to those ahead.

They turned, and, huddling together in the storm, they looked at one another with scared faces.

"I warned you to keep close together," began Joshua, but forbore to chide, as he saw the dumb agony in the eyes of the other two men.

"Turn back," said Shelby, "and quickly. How long do you suppose he has been gone? Has he missed the track? What happened, Joshua?"

"He must have fallen," the guide replied. "Or maybe just strayed off, blinded by the snow, and he's wandering around yet. He has a compass and he knows where to head for. Small use our trying to turn back and find him. He's 'way off by this time,—or, maybe, he ain't. Maybe he's close behind,—we couldn't see him ten yards off in this snow."

"I never saw such a thickness of white!" exclaimed Blair. "I've heard that when snow is so white and feathery, it doesn't last long."

"This snow does," returned Joshua, "and I tell you, Mr. Shelby, there's no use turning back. We'd just waste our time,—maybe our lives——"

"But, man, we can't go without Crane!" Shelby cried. "I won't go on and leave him to his fate!"

"'Tain't likely he's in any real danger," said Joshua, almost believing his own statement. "If it was one of you two, now, I'd feel more alarmed. But Mr. Crane,—he's got a head on him, and a compass, and he knows the route we're taking,—he went over it with me before we started. Lord knows I'd be the first one to go to his rescue, if it was rescue he needed, but I don't think it is."

"Rescue or not," said Blair, "I will not go on without Peter. You two do what you like. I'm going to turn back and hunt for him."

"So am I," declared Shelby, and the two turned to face the backward trail.

"All foolishness," muttered Joshua, "but of course, I'll go along."

It was all foolishness, there was no doubt of that. The snow had covered all signs of their own tracks, there was no road to follow, no landmarks to go by. Though Joshua had pursued his route by compass, he could not retrace it surely enough to find a lost man.

However, they persisted; they dashed at snow-covered mounds only to find them hummocks or rocks. They hallooed and shouted; they stared into the snowy distance, hoping to discern smoke; but though their big, strong Peter was less than half a mile away from them, they could get no hint of his presence.

Night came on. They built their camp fire of enormous dimensions, hoping against hope that it might attract the lost man.

None slept, save for a few fitful dozes from sheer exhaustion and grief. Joshua stolidly insisted that Peter was undoubtedly all right, and though they could scarcely believe it, this comforted the other two.

Next morning they held council. Joshua was all for going on and giving up the search for Crane.

Blair, too, felt it a useless waste of time to remain, but Shelby begged for a few hours.

"If the storm abates just a little——" he began.

"It won't," declared Joshua. "It's a little mite less windy but this snowfall's only just begun. It won't quit for days,—lessen it turns to rain,—and then the goin''ll be a heap worse."

It didn't seem as if the going could be much worse. Already the men had difficulty in moving because of their wet, half-frozen clothing. Available wood was buried under the snow, their strength was becoming impaired, and all things pointed to even worse weather conditions.

Reluctantly Shelby and Blair agreed to Joshua's plans, realizing that Peter might be all right and on his homeward journey, and further delay might result in their own loss of life. For the outlook was menacing, and Joshua's knowledge and advice were sincere and authoritative.

And still it snowed. Steadily, persistently, uninterruptedly. There seemed a permanency about that soft, downward moving mass that foreboded danger and defeat to any one who remained to dare it further.

And so they started again, half glad to go, half unwilling to leave. It was the terrible uncertainty that told on them. They shrank from facing the thought of what it would mean if they didn't find Peter, and forced themselves to believe that they would meet him.

Their objective point was a trapper's log house on the shore of the lake.

They reached it, tired, footsore, but full of hope for good news. A quick glance round the tiny interior, consisting of but two rooms, showed no smiling-faced Peter.

A few words from Joshua to the trappers gave no cause for rejoicing, and further conversation and explanation revealed the fact that the experienced trappers had no doubt as to Peter's fate.

Nor did they blame Joshua in any way. Had he stayed for a longer search, they averred, there would have been four dead men instead of one.

And then both Shelby and Blair realized that Joshua's expressed hopefulness of finding Peter safe at the end of their journey was merely by way of urging them to move on, knowing the result if they did not.

They also realized that he was right. The opinions and assertions of the experienced trappers could not be gainsaid. The two came to know that there was but one fate that could have overtaken their comrade and that there was no hope possible.

If Shelby had a slight feeling that Blair ought to have looked back oftener, he gave it no voice, for he knew he himself had never looked back with any idea of watching over Blair. To be sure the last one of the four was in the most dangerous position, but Peter had come last by mere chance, and no one had given that point a thought.

They surmised something must have disabled him. Perhaps a cramp or a fainting spell of exhaustion. But it was necessarily only surmise, and one theory was as tenable as another.

Long parleys were held by Blair and Shelby as to what was best to be done. It proved to be impossible to persuade any one to start on a search for the body of Crane. The winter had set in and it was a hopeless task to undertake in the snows of the wild. No, they were told, not until March at the earliest, could a search be undertaken, and there was small chance of finding the body until later spring melted the snow. It was to be an especially bad winter, all agreed, and no pleas, bribes or threats of the men could move the natives from their decision.

Then, they debated, should they go home, or wait till spring?

The latter plan seemed foolish, for it was now nearly November and to wait there idly for five or six months was appalling. Moreover, it seemed their duty to go home and report Peter's loss to his father, even if they returned in the spring to search for the body of their chum.

The last boat left for Newfoundland the middle of November, and they concluded that if there was no news of Peter by that time they would sail on it. "I feel cowardly to go," said Shelby, whose brain was weary, working out the problem of duty. "Yet, why stay?"

"It's right to go," Blair said, gravely. "You see, Mr. Crane must be *told*,—not written to."

"One of us might go,—and one stay," Shelby suggested.

"No use in that," Blair said, after a moment's consideration; "the remaining one couldn't do anything."

"You men talk foolishness," said Joshua, gravely. "Mr. Peter Crane is by this time buried under eight feet of snow. You can do nothing. You'd both better go home."

So they went.

CHAPTER 4: THE PROPHECY RECALLED

The steamer from Newfoundland that brought Shelby and Blair to New York arrived during Christmas week.

The two men, however, were far from feeling holiday cheer as they reached the wharf and faced the hard trial of telling Mr. and Mrs. Crane of their son's death.

But it had to be done, and they felt it their duty to lose no time in performing the sad errand.

No one met them at the steamer, for its hour of arrival was uncertain and they had discouraged their friends from the attempt.

Indeed only telegrams from Newfoundland had apprised any one of their arrival, for letters would have come by the same boat they came themselves.

"Let's go straight to the Cranes' and get it over," said Blair; with a sigh. "I dread the ordeal."

"So do I," Shelby confessed. "I wish we could see Mr. Crane alone, first."

"We must do that, of course. It's only eight o'clock, and we're ready to start now. Come ahead."

They sent their luggage to their homes and took a taxi for the Crane town house, on upper Park Avenue.

By good fortune, Mr. Crane was at home and received them in his library. They had asked to see him alone, giving no names.

"My stars, if it isn't the wanderers returned!" exclaimed their host, as he entered and saw the two. "Where's my boy? Hiding behind the window curtain?"

But the expression on his visitors' faces suddenly checked his speech, and turning pale, Benjamin Crane dropped into the nearest chair.

"What is it?" he whispered, in a shaking voice. "I know it's bad news. Is Peter——"

"Yes," said Shelby, gently, but feeling that the shortest statement was most merciful. "The Labrador got him."

By a strange locution, Labrador, as we call it, is spoken of up there as The Labrador, and the phrase gives a sinister sound to the name. It personifies it, and makes it seem like a living menace, a sentient danger.

"Tell me about it," said Benjamin Crane, and his tense, strained voice told more of his grief than any outburst could have done.

*   *   *   *   *

"Lost in the snow! My little Peter Boots——" he said, after he had listened in silence to their broken recital. "Tell me more," he urged, and eagerly drank in any details they could give him of the tragedy and also of the doings of the party before that last, fatal day.

Blair looked at him in secret amazement. How could the man take it so calmly? But Shelby, a deeper student of human character, understood how the fearful shock of tragedy had stunned the loving father-heart. Slowly and quietly, Shelby related many incidents of the trip, drew word pictures of Peter in his gayest moods, told tales of his courage, bravery and unfailing good spirits.

But, though these things interested Crane and held his attention, there was no way to lessen the poignant sorrow of the last story,—the account of the terrible storm and the awful fate of Peter.

Shelby broke down, and Blair finished, with a few broken sentences.

The deep grief of the two, the sincere love of Peter and sorrow at his death proved better than protestations that they had done all mortal effort could do.

"I am not sure, sir," Shelby said, finally, "that we acted wisely, but it seemed the only course to take. We could not persuade any one to go for us or with us in search of Peter's body, until March at the earliest. To go alone, was mere suicide, and though I was tempted to do even that, rather than to return without him, it would not have been allowed."

"Oh, I understand perfectly," Crane said, quickly, "I wouldn't have had you do otherwise than just as you did. There was no use trying the impossible."

"But we will return in March——" began Blair.

"Perhaps," said Crane, a little preoccupied in manner, "or I will send a search party myself. There's no reason you boys should go."

This was a real relief, for though more than willing, the two men were far from anxious to undertake the gruesome errand.

"And now," their host went on, "if you agree, I'll send for Mrs. Crane. At first, I thought I'd rather tell her the news when we were by ourselves,—but, I know there are questions she will want to ask you, things that I might not think of,—and I know you'll be willing to answer her."

All unconscious of the scene awaiting her, Mrs. Crane came into the room.

A bewildered look on her sweet, placid face showed her inability to grasp the situation quickly.

Then, "Why, boys," she cried, "when did you come home? Where's Peter?"

To the others' relief Benjamin Crane told his wife of their mutual loss. Very gently he told her, very lovingly he held her hand and comforted her crushed and breaking heart. Shelby and Blair instinctively turned aside from the pitiful scene and waited to be again addressed.

At length Mrs. Crane turned her tear-stained face to them. Not so calm as her husband, she begged for details, then she wept and sobbed so hysterically she could scarcely hear them. Her thoughts flew back to the years when Peter was a lad, a child, a baby,—and her talk of him became almost incoherent.

"There, there, dear," Benjamin Crane said, smoothing her hair, "try to be quieter,—you will make yourself ill.

Perhaps, boys, you'd better go now, and come round again
to-morrow evening."

"No, no!" cried Mrs. Crane; "stay longer,—tell me
more. Tell me everything he said or did,—all the time you
were gone. Did he know he was going to die?"

"Oh, no, Mrs. Crane," Shelby assured her. "It was an
accident, you see. The storm was beyond anything you
can imagine. The wind was not only icy and cutting, but
of a sharp viciousness that made it impossible to hear or
to see. Almost impossible to walk. We merely struggled
blindly against it,—*against* it, you understand, so that if
Peter, who was behind, had called out, we could not have
heard him."

"Why was he last?" demanded Mrs. Crane.

"It happened so," replied Shelby. "I've tried hard to
think if we were to blame for that,—but I cannot see that
we were. Whenever we walked single file, we fell into line
in any order. The subject never was mentioned or thought
of. And so, that day, Peter was the last one. If Blair or I
had fallen or been overcome by the cold,—which is what
we know must have happened,—we would have been seen
by Peter, of course. But when he gave out, no one looked
backward."

"You had been trudging like that long?" asked Crane.

"Oh, yes, for hours. We were all pretty nearly all in,
but Joshua wouldn't let us stop,—dared not, in fact, for he
knew the danger of that storm far better than we did. No,
Mr. Crane, on the part of Blair and myself, I want to say
that we had no thought other than our individual
progress. That was all any one could think of, as Peter
himself would say if he could speak."

"He has spoken," returned Crane, quietly; "he did say
it."

"What!" exclaimed the two men together.

"Yes," the older man went on; "I think I will tell you,
though I had half decided not to: What do you say,
Mother?"

Mrs. Crane looked up. Her expression of dumb despair gave way to a look of quiet peace as she said, slowly: "Yes, dear, tell them. But let it be held confidential."

"You'll promise that, boys, won't you?" asked Crane, and only half understanding Blair and Shelby promised.

"Well, it was this way," Crane began, "You know we couldn't get letters from you chaps all the time you were away,—except the few early ones. Of course we knew that before you went, but we didn't realize how lonely we would be without Peter Boots. Whenever he has been away before we could hear from him frequently. Julie is a dear girl, but she is a busy little butterfly, and many a time my wife and I are alone of an evening."

"And we're happy enough together," Mrs. Crane put in, gently; "but being alone, we naturally talked a great deal of Peter, and—and we couldn't help remembering the Gypsy's warning."

"Oh, I'd forgotten that!" exclaimed Blair. "What was it, now?"

"A prophecy that Peter would go on a long journey, and would meet with a terrible death. Now, the prophecy is fulfilled." Mrs. Crane's face, as she gazed upward, her eyes filled with tears, was like that of a seeress or prophetess. She appeared exalted, and unconscious of her grief for the moment.

"And there was further prophecy," Benjamin Crane continued, "that after his death, Peter would return. And when I say he has done so, I expect you to respect my story and not to doubt its truth."

"We shall most certainly respect your story, and no one could doubt your veracity, Mr. Crane," said Shelby, sincerely, though with a mental reservation that believing in Benjamin Crane's veracity did not necessarily mean subscribing to his hallucinations.

Blair's face showed his interest and curiosity, and Benjamin Crane went on with the tale to a breathlessly absorbed audience.

"It did come about, I've no doubt, because of our talks of Peter; and also, because we chanced to hear of some neighbors who had wonderful success with a Ouija Board."

A sudden, involuntary exclamation on the part of Blair was immediately suppressed by a warning glance from Shelby. It would never do to show scorn of the Ouija Board and all its works in the presence of this afflicted couple. If any comfort from its use had reached them or could reach them, it must be a blessing indeed.

"Yes," Crane said, catching the meaning of the look on Blair's face, "I know how you feel about such things, but just reserve judgment until you hear our experiences. We bought a Board, and mother and I tried to use it alone. We had no success at all. It would spell nothing coherent,—only meaningless jumbles of letters,—or simply refuse to move. Of course, you understand, we had no thought that our boy was—was in any danger,—but we had been told that sometimes living persons communicated by such means. So we persevered, but we never got a message."

"Then what happened?" asked Blair, eagerly, seeing from the faces of the older people that something had.

"Why then," Mrs. Crane spoke now,—"we found somebody to help us. I'd rather not tell the name,—it was a lady——"

"A medium?" asked Shelby.

"Oh, no! I mean, not a professional medium,—a lady we've known for years. She had had some experience with the Board, and she tried it with us. And then,—you tell it, father."

"Then," said Mr. Crane, speaking very seriously, "then we got a message from Peter. The message said that he had died in the snow."

"What!" cried Shelby, "incredible! When was this?"

"In November."

"Peter died the seventeenth of October."

"Yes, and it was the tenth of November that we had the message."

"Just what did it say?" asked Blair, his eyes wide with amazement.

"It was a little stammering and uncertain, as if hard to get it through. But the Ouija spelled out Peter's name, and when she—Miss—when the lady with us asked if it had a message from Peter, it pointed to 'yes.' Then she tried to get the message. But the words were a little mixed up. There was *snow* and *ice* and *storm* and at last the word *dead*. When we asked if Peter had died in a snowstorm the Board said yes. So, we knew the prophecy was fulfilled at last. The news you brought us was corroboration, not a surprise."

Shelby restrained himself by an effort. His sharp glance at Blair made him keep quiet also. Neither was at all impressed at the story Crane told them, except to be moved to ridicule. Well they knew how a Ouija Board will make glib statements as startling as they are untrue.

But this one happened to be true. Even so, the fact of its relation by such means was unbelievable to both the hearers.

Yet, they could not disturb the faith of the parents of their lost chum.

"I am glad, for your sakes, that you had a premonitory warning," said Shelby, in all sincerity. "Such things are indeed beyond our ken. Did you get any further details?"

"No," said Crane; "but, I learn, you have no further details yourselves. My boy perished in the snowstorm, alone and helpless. What more is there to know?"

"Nothing that we could tell," spoke up Blair, a little excitedly, "but surely, the spirit of Peter,—if it was he speaking to you,—could have told more!"

"It is clear you have had no experience in these matters," Crane said, mildly; "the messages are not easy to get, nor are they concise and clear, like a telegram. Only occasionally does one get through, and then if it is informative we are duly grateful,—and not dissatisfied and clamoring for more."

"I beg your pardon, Mr. Crane; I am inexperienced, but I assure you I am not a scoffer. And of course, I believe your statements."

"Of course!" exclaimed Mrs. Crane, a little crisply. "Surely we would not invent such a story!"

"No, indeed," said Shelby. "It is strange, you must admit. Have you had any further communications from Peter?"

"A few," Mr. Crane spoke a bit reluctantly, for he could see that the men were receptive from a motive of politeness, and not with sympathetic interest. "He has sent other messages, but they would not, I fear, convince you."

"Now, don't blame us, Mr. Crane," Blair broke out, impetuously; "remember, we're just from the place where we left Peter,—remember, we love him, too,—and remember, if we could be convinced that he had spoken we would be as interested as you are."

"Well put, my boy," and Crane seemed greatly mollified. "Now, merely as an admission of facts, do you believe that the Ouija Board gave the messages exactly as I have detailed the proceedings to you?"

"I do," said Blair, "that is, I believe you have told the exact truth of what you observed."

"Then, can you refuse to believe that the message came from the spirit of my dead boy? Who else knew of his death? How could any one know of it?"

"True enough," and Blair shook his head, noncommittally.

Crane sighed. "You don't believe," he said, but without annoyance. "Yet, remember, greater minds and wiser brains than yours believe. Are not you a little presumptuous to set your opinion against theirs?"

"I don't mean to be presumptuous, Mr. Crane," Blair spoke decidedly, "but I do think my opinion on this subject as good as any man's."

"Then you are condemning the matter, unheard, which you will allow is not strictly just."

"Come, come, Blair," said Shelby, distressed at his attitude, "don't discuss things of which you know nothing. Mr. Crane has gone deeply into the subject and must know more about it than we do." He gave Blair a positive glance of reproof, and tried to make him see that he must stop combating their host's theories, if only for reasons of common politeness.

"But I'm interested," persisted Blair. "If Peter came here and told his father he was dead,— I want to look into these things. You see, it's the first time I've ever been up against a real case of this sort. Own up, Shelby, it's all mighty queer."

Benjamin Crane looked kindly at Blair. "That's the talk, my boy. If you're really interested, come round some night, and with you here, Peter may talk through, all the better."

"Rubbish!" Shelby thought, silently, but aloud, he only said:

"Yes, Blair, do that. And drop the subject for the present. Is Julie at home, Mrs. Crane?"

"No; she's away for a few days. Poor child, she will be heartbroken. She adored Peter Boots," and Mrs. Crane again gave way to tears.

"What does Julie think about the messages?" asked Blair, thoughtfully.

"We didn't tell her," said Crane. "She's so emotional, and—well, of course, we couldn't help hoping that it mightn't be true. And, too, Julie hates all talk of spiritism."

"Sensible girl!" thought Shelby, as Mrs. Crane was saying:

"But Julie went to Sir Rowland's lectures and she was deeply interested."

"Lectures?" asked Blair.

"Yes; there have been a great many this season. I'm sorry you had to miss them. They're over now. But I can't see how any one could listen to that delightful man talk on such subjects in his beautiful way and not be convinced of the truth of it all."

"What did he say?" asked Shelby.

"That's too big a question to be answered in a sentence," and Crane smiled a little, "but he gave us incontrovertible proof that the spirits of the dead return and communicate with their friends who are still on earth."

"Through a Ouija Board?" Blair inquired.

"Yes; and by actual manifestation as well. I've never consulted a real medium, but now that I know Peter is gone, I shall do so."

"Don't!" Shelby said, quite involuntarily. Then, seeing the look in Crane's eyes, he added: "Forgive me, sir, I have no right to advise. But I've been told that all professional mediums are frauds."

"We are told many things,—both for and against," returned Crane, "but if Sir Rowland is willing to consult them, and believes in them, I'm ready to sail under his flag."

"Of course. And you've a perfect right to do so." Shelby felt he couldn't control his real opinions much longer, and wanted to go. "May I come to see you again, soon,—and talk over the matters of Peter's things,—which, of course, we brought home? And, I'd like to see Julie."

"She'll be home by to-morrow evening. Of course, we'll send for her. And I know she'll want to see you both. Perhaps not just at first, but after a few days. Please come to the house whenever you will,—just as you used to do."

"Yes, do," added Mrs. Crane, her lip quivering at the remembrance of the old days when the boys were jolly together.

"And Miss Harper, how is she?" asked Blair, who had been longing to put the question for some time.

"Well, as usual," replied Mrs. Crane. "She was here last night. She——"

"She's a dear girl," Crane interrupted his wife, and a peculiar look crossed his face. "You come round soon again, boys, but I fear we must let you go now. My wife is keeping up bravely, but——" he glanced at the little woman tenderly, and took her hand in his. "And I, too, don't feel like talking more now. So good-night,—and, thank you for all your good comradeship with my boy,— my Peter Boots."

"We want sympathy, too, Mr. Crane," said Blair; "Peter was very dear to us both. We're not given to spilling over, but we have lost a dear friend and chum whose place can never be filled by another."

"Right!" said Shelby, in a choked voice, and his handclasp with Peter's father said the rest.

But once on the street his exasperation broke forth in words. "I can stand any sort of idiots," he said, "except spook idiots! They make me want to go back to the Labrador!"

"Sort of queer, though, that message,—from Peter—— "

"From Peter—nothing! Don't desecrate that boy's memory by even an implication that he'd fiddle with a Ouija Board! Ugh!"

"How do you explain it, then?"

"There's nothing to explain."

"You think Crane,—er—misstated?"

"Oh, I think he thought he had a message,—but he was duped. They all are. I know all about that Sir Rowland. I've read his books. He's dotty on the subject. Keep off the rocks, Blair. You've a leaning that way, and if you don't look out you'll fall for it, too."

"Wonder why Mr. Crane shut his wife up when she started to say something about Carly Harper."

"Oh, that was nothing particular. Anyway, you can see Carly for yourself. I expect she'll be hard hit by Peter's death. They were practically engaged."

"How'd you know?"

"Peter told me,—not in words, bless his heart! He just let it out when he was in a babbling mood. I mean, he let fall side remarks, and I just gathered the truth. I didn't tell him I knew. Open-hearted as he was, Peter was reserved in some ways."

"Dear old chap, so he was. Our great work will never materialize now. Unless I write it alone. I'd like to do that,—and publish it over both our names, and explain in a preface."

"Do," said Shelby; "it would please the old people a lot."

CHAPTER 5: MADAME PARLATO

Blair's first interview with Carly Harper was painful for both. The Cranes had told her of Peter's death, but the sight of Blair seemed to bring home to the girl a further and more vivid realization of her loss.

"I wish now I'd been kinder to him," she said, her voice quivering.

"Oh, come now, Carly, I know you weren't unkind."

"No; but I wouldn't—wouldn't do what he asked me——"

"Never mind, dear; I think I know what you mean, and, let me tell you, old Peter was happy enough—about you. He seemed pretty sure that things were coming his way."

"Of course," the girl said frankly. "I only wanted him to go away, free, and then if he still wanted me when he came back—and now he'll never come back!" she gave way to silent weeping.

"His parents say he has come back," offered Blair, more by way of diversion than comfort.

Carly looked up quickly. "They told you that?" she said.

"Yes, told me pretty much all about their 'messages.' Foolishness, of course, but it seems to comfort them."

"It doesn't comfort me," and Carly sighed. "I don't believe in it, you see." And she looked at him with a curious glance.

"No; I don't either. But the old people do, and if it helps them bear their grief,—why——"

"Yes; I understand. How—how much did they tell you?"

"All, I suppose. They said some medium,—well, not a professional, but some friend of theirs,—helped them to get messages 'through,' as they call it."

"Didn't they tell you who the friend was?"

"No; but they weren't mysterious about it. They simply didn't say. I believe Julie doesn't like to have them try it,—the Ouija, I mean."

"Oh, she feels as I do,—as anybody must,—if they like it let them have it. She went to the lectures."

"Everybody did, it seems."

"Yes, the whole town went crazy on the subject. Is yet, but not quite to the same extent."

"The war brought it all about, of course. After a short time, the fad will die out."

"Yes, if it is a fad. But,—do you never think there may be a grain of truth in it all?"

"I haven't seen the grain yet, but I'm open to conviction."

"Oh, well, I've no intention of trying to convince you. Tell me all about your trip,—tell me all the queer experiences you had, and everything you can think of. And tell me lots about Peter."

Blair did her bidding. He described their life in the Labrador, told of their exploits and discomforts and also of the glorious outdoor days and nights that were so enjoyed by them all.

"I'd love it!" Carly declared. "Oh, not all the tramping and portaging, but the camp life."

"Better try it nearer home. The Adirondacks would give you enough excitement. There's no use braving that cold up there, and those fierce storms."

"If it hadn't stormed, Peter wouldn't have been lost, would he?"

"Probably not. You see, we've mulled it over and over. He must have fallen and hurt himself in some way, or he would have followed us somehow."

"He would have called out."

"That's the point. The wind was in our faces, it was a villainous blast, and nothing any one said could be heard by one in front of him, unless they were near each other. If Peter had shouted, the wind would have carried his voice back and away from us. That is undoubtedly what happened."

"Don't you think the guide was greatly to blame?"

"No; he had no reason to look back at us, as if we were sheep. We had always followed his trail, there was to all appearances no difference between this trip and any other. We had breasted equally severe storms, and come home, laughing. I feel sure Peter met with an accident,—or, it may be,—probably enough,—his strength suddenly gave out, or even his heart went bad, or something like that. Perhaps he couldn't shout. I blame myself, of course, for not looking back sooner, but I do honestly feel that it was not a culpable omission."

"Of course it wasn't! I see just how it was. Great, big, stalwart Peter was not a baby to be looked after by you others. But—oh, Gilbert,—it's so dreadful to think of his dying there alone! Perhaps he—he didn't die right away——"

"Don't, Carly! Try not to think about that. Think only that old Peter Boots is gone,—that he lived a fine, clean, splendid life, and met his end bravely, whatever happened. And, too, I'm told that he couldn't have suffered much. He must have lost consciousness very quickly."

"Yes,—I suppose so. But—oh, Gilbert, I didn't know how much I cared, until—until I lost him."

"I know, dear,—it's awful hard for you. Come on, get your hat and let's go over to Julie's. I haven't seen her yet, and I promised to call to-day."

They went to the Cranes', and found Shelby already there.

It was tea hour, and several people were gathered about Julie's pretty tea table.

For the Crane family, though in mourning, received gladly the intimate friends who had loved Peter, and who came, full of sympathy, to talk of him.

Julie received Blair with a warm welcome, but,—or at least so Blair thought,—she was a little cool in her greeting to Carlotta.

The two girls were pleasant enough, but there was an evident constraint between them, and both turned quickly aside to talk to some one else.

Blair pondered. He was by way of noting significant details and his own interest in Carly Harper made him quick to resent any slight put upon her. Not that Julie's attitude could be called really slighting, nor was it more so than Carly's own, but there was some dissonance there.

His observation, though veiled by a pleasant, general interest in everything, was no less acute, and he continued to note that the girls really avoided each other. It was none of his business, but he was curious and surprised at a state of affairs so different from the intimacy he had known them to enjoy of old.

He bided his time, and at last, finding an opportunity, he spoke to Julie alone. She still sat at the tea table, but all having been served, she was idle and a little distrait.

"I'm glad to see you again, Gilbert," she said, at last, looking at him through tearful eyes, "but it makes me think of Peter, and—oh, talk,—or I shall go all to pieces!"

Knowing Julie's emotional nature, Blair tactfully talked, telling Peter's sister of trifling occurrences that were interesting in themselves rather than of personal import. He succeeded in restoring her calm and at last a chance allusion brought up Carly's name.

"What's the trouble between you two girls?" Blair asked, lightly.

"Trouble? There isn't any," and Julie's blue eyes,—so like Peter's,—looked straight at him.

"Oh, just a school-girl squabble, is it?"

"It isn't anything," Julie persisted, "why do you say that?"

"Now, look here, Julie Crane, you can't fool me. I'm a mind reader, and I see there's a rift in the lute that you and Carly used to play duets on."

Julie smiled at the way he put it, and said, half unwillingly: "Well, you see, Gilbert, Carly's a snake-in-the-grass."

"What! Oh, I say, Julie, don't talk like that! What do you mean?"

"She's underhanded, sly, deceitful, dishonest——"

"Stop, stop! You're losing your mind! Suppose you let up on vituperation and do a bit of explaining. What has Carly done to merit those terms?"

"What has she done? She has come over here,—when I've been away,—and stirred up father and mother with that silly, hateful, vicious old Ouija Board performance,—that's what she's done!"

"Ouija! Carly! Surely you're mistaken."

"Indeed, I'm not. Father and mother couldn't make the silly thing go at all, till Carly helped them. She pushes it, of course,—and they are gulled and duped——"

"But, Julie, wait! Why should Carly do such a thing?"

"Oh, she's got the fad. Lots of people have, you know. And I haven't—I hate it all—and so Carly comes over when I'm not home."

"And was it she who got the messages from Peter?"

"Yes, it was; that is, she pretended to."

Blair was amazed. Carly had given him the impression that she didn't believe in occult manifestations. Why should she do that, if she had assisted at the Crane *seances*? He hated to think of Carlotta Harper as insincere, but—he mused—that sort of thing tends to make people insincere. He came to a quick decision that he would observe for himself and not seek further enlightenment directly from either of the two girls.

So he only said, carelessly, "There's no accounting for the doings of people who are obsessed by that sort of thing. But, look here, Julie, if it is any comfort to your parents to think they have messages from Peter, you wouldn't disturb their belief, would you?"

"No, I don't. That's why I don't have a real quarrel with Carly. I think she knows I've discovered her part in it all, and I think she knows I resent it; but, as you say, if it helps dear old dad and mother to bear their grief, I'm willing they should wear out one Ouija Board after another!"

"Good girl. You attended the lectures, I hear."

"Yes, and they meant nothing to me. What was produced as evidence seemed to me no evidence at all. I'd like your honest opinion, Gilbert."

"I didn't hear the lectures."

"But you can read the books. Sir Rowland has written several, and there are hundreds of others. Do read some, and see if you can find anything in them—anything at all that is conclusive proof."

"Proof of what? Of continuity of existence?"

"Not that, no. But proof that the spirits of the dead have ever communicated with the living."

It was during this conversation that Benjamin Crane came in. He was evidently in a happy mood, his face was radiant and his fine features glowed with enthusiasm.

"I've had such an experience," he exclaimed. "I've had a *seance* with a real medium——"

"Oh, father!" Julie cried out, involuntarily, but he only smiled benignly at her.

"Just listen, Julie, dear. Reserve your comment till you hear it all. Then we'll see."

He drew his armchair nearer the fire and rubbed his hands to the blaze, then settled back in comfort, taking the cup that Julie brought him.

"Yes, yes," he went on, "a wonderful experience. You know," he looked round, including all his hearers, for all present had drawn near to listen, "you know I felt sure we had no real mediums here in America. When Sir Rowland told of the trustworthy ones he has consulted in England, I almost decided to go over there myself. But I heard of one here in New York, and I investigated fully her credentials and references before going to her. Truly, she is a marvel."

"I thought they weren't allowed," observed Shelby, smiling a little.

"'Not allowed' is sometimes a mere figure of speech," and Mr. Crane smiled, too. "However, I was allowed to see her and have a real *seance*—oh, Helen," he turned to his wife, "I can scarcely wait to go there again and have you go with me."

"Father, I can't stand this!" Julie's eyes were blazing. "Please drop the subject—at least, for the present."

"There, there, my daughter, don't lose your temper. If you don't want to hear about this, you may be excused." He smiled at her lovingly but with a decided intention.

"You're all interested, are you not?" he went on, turning to the various attentive faces, and receiving nods and words of assent.

"Then I'll go on," and he glanced at Julie, who sat still, controlling her expression of face but with tumult in her heart.

"Take it easy," Shelby whispered to her, "you'd better hear it, you know, whatever it's all about."

"The lady," Crane said, "is a medium, well recommended by members of the Society for Psychical Research, and by individuals who have been her clients."

"What sort of recommendations does she offer?" asked an interested voice, "letters?"

The speaker was McClellan Thorpe, a friend of Blair's, who shared a studio with him.

Thorpe was frankly skeptical, but by no means controversial. He asked his question in an honest desire to know of the credentials.

"Yes," returned Crane, "letters from many well-known Spiritists, Psychics, Scientists and plain citizens, who are enthusiastic and sincere in their praise of this lady."

"What's her name?" asked Mrs. Crane, who, it was plain to be seen, fairly hung upon her husband's words.

"Madame Parlato," returned Crane. "She is no fraud, no charlatan, but a refined, gracious lady, whose sympathies are as wonderful as her occult gifts."

Carlotta Harper, who sat by Thorpe, was absorbed in the tale, and her large dark eyes glowed, with intense interest as she listened.

"Tell us just what happened," she said, and Julie gave her a look of mingled scorn and apprehension.

"I will," Crane's deep voice went on. "The lady, you understand, knew nothing of me or of Peter. I was careful about this, for I know there are unscrupulous mediums, and I wanted to feel sure of this one's honesty."

"How do you know she'd never heard of you?" asked Thorpe. He had a manner of speaking that was definite without being annoying. Apparently he was curious, and not, necessarily, incredulous.

"How could she?" returned Crane, "we have no mutual friends. I heard of her through a comparative stranger, and I went to her at once. Don't be carping, Thorpe, just wait till you hear my story. Well, she greeted me pleasantly, and with a most courteous and lady-like demeanor. I had an appointment, of course, and she directed me to sit at a table opposite herself. I did so, and for quite a time nothing happened.

"Then—she was not exactly in a trance, I should say, but rather she seemed absorbed in deep thought—she said, 'I see a man, a fair-haired man with a sunny, boyish smile. Do you recognize that description?' I didn't say much, for I'm no fool to give myself away, you understand, but I nodded assent, and she went on: 'He seems very active, full of life and energy, and of a loving, affectionate nature.' You may guess how I felt when she described Peter so exactly! I wanted to exclaim, 'Yes, that's my boy!' but I'm always careful not to help in any way. So I just nodded, and she went on. 'He passed away about two or three months ago, and he seems willing to communicate with me. What shall I ask him?'

"Now, I'm canny, you know, and I said, 'Make sure of his identity first. Ask him what name we used to call him by?' And, will you believe it? after a short pause, she said, 'Peter Boots!' She seemed surprised herself at such a name. I thought I ought to tell her how true that was, so I did. She looked pleased to think it was all right, and waited for me to ask another question. So I said, 'Ask him how he died.' She did, and he told her he was frozen to death in a fearful snowstorm. Think of that! And I said, 'Ask him how it happened.' And she did, and Peter said he couldn't exactly say—he lost consciousness, and he knew nothing more until he found himself on the other side. He said for me not to grieve, for he should carry on over there all he had attempted to do here. He said he retained all his ambition and energy and hope—you know he was blessed abundantly with those traits—and——"

"Did he say he was happy?" asked Mrs. Crane, eagerly.

"He said he was content, and though it was all a little strange as yet, he was becoming accustomed to that life and did not wish to return."

"Did he send any message to me?" urged the anxious mother.

"I'm coming to that, dear. Yes, he said for you not to grieve for him, but to think of him as busy and happy and entirely contented. Oh, Helen, isn't it wonderful? I arranged for another *seance*, and you shall go with me. She held out a hope of materialization later, but she wasn't sure she could compass that for some time to come. You needn't look skeptical, Thorpe; that expression on your face only proves your ignorance of these things. I tell you, man, if it were somebody you loved and cherished you'd be mighty glad to hear from him!"

"Never mind my expression, Mr. Crane," Thorpe
returned, looking apologetic, "I'm deeply interested, I can
tell you, and I'd like to hear more."

"There's little more to tell. It was a quiet session—
none of that curtained cabinet, tambourine-playing
business, you understand; but a plain revelation from my
boy's spirit through the medium of a refined, cultured
woman. I'm sorry, now, I didn't take my wife with me to-
day, but I feared it might not be so agreeable, and I tried
it out myself first. But we will go together soon."

Crane beamed happily, and it was impossible not to
rejoice with him in his delight and satisfaction at his
experience.

Julie, her lips pressed tightly together, made no
comment on her father's story. Christopher Shelby, who
sat beside her, eyed her covertly, not quite decided
whether to speak to her on the subject or not.

He concluded to do so, and whispered, "How does it all
strike you?"

"I don't know," she returned, passing her hand across
her white brow with a wearied gesture. "If it had been
those foolish cabinet affairs I should have been disgusted,
but the really nice woman,—as father describes her,—and
he never misrepresents,—gives a slightly different face on
it. Still, I can't believe——"

"Shall you go to the next *seance*?"

"I haven't been asked. I doubt if they'll want me. I
wonder what Carly thinks of it all."

But Carlotta was talking with Blair and Mr. Thorpe,
and their conversation had no connection with the subject
in hand. They were discussing a wedding of two of their
mutual friends, which had proved a surprise to them all.
Blair and Julie joined that discussion, and the matter of
the *seance* was not again referred to by the young people.

But on the way home Thorpe spoke his mind to Blair,
who accompanied him.

"How can a sensible, otherwise well-balanced man
like Benjamin Crane fall for that fake?" he exclaimed.

"I've known Mr. Crane for years and he never showed signs of paresis before!"

"I don't attempt to explain it," returned Blair, casually, "but I do know that lots of other equally hard-headed citizens are tarred with the same brush."

"That's true enough, but this is the first time I've run up against it so closely. I say, Blair, how did the lingo tally with the facts of Peter's death? Or would you rather not talk about it?"

"I don't mind talking about it at all. Why should I, among Peter's friends? As to facts, we know none ourselves except that he was lost in the snow. You've no idea of that snow, Thorpe! It was like a thick, white feather-bed, falling, falling continually. It was impenetrable to sight or hearing. The wind blew it about some, but it fell so thickly that it seemed a solid mass that we struggled through. And it was quite all we could do to get along——"

"Oh, don't think for a minute I feel you were in the least derelict! I know you weren't. It merely chanced that Peter's heart gave out—or whatever it was that did happen—while he was the last one of the procession."

"And not only that. If, say, I'd fallen, a man behind might not have seen me go down. If we swerved ever so little from a straight line, and, of course, we did,—couldn't help it,—we lost sight for a moment of the man in front. And as we all went along, eyes down or closed much of the time, we might have lost a man who wasn't walking last. I wish I could make you see it, Mac! See the traveling, I mean. I've never progressed against such difficulties."

"I know, old chap. Do get out of your head that anybody blames any of you in the least. And if they did, the blame would fall on the guide, not on you fellows."

"Joshua was not a bit to blame either. Surely you see that. It was every man for himself,—and—fate took the hindmost! Oh, I hate to think about it! It's even worse to me now than when it happened. The more I think about it the more I grieve for dear old Peter. We were good pals, you know."

"I know it; we all were. Mighty few chaps like Peter Boots!"

CHAPTER 6: STRANGE REVELATIONS

"Old man Crane's gone nutty," Shelby remarked.

"Been going for some time," agreed Blair, and McClellan Thorpe nodded his head decidedly.

The three sat in the studio apartment occupied by Blair and Thorpe, who had just returned from dining at their club.

Shelby had come home with them, but was soon to leave to keep an engagement.

"You'll scarcely believe what I'm up to to-night," Shelby went on, "I'm going to a *seance* with Mr. Crane."

"I say, Kit," remonstrated Thorpe, "I don't think you ought to encourage him. He's daft enough on the subject now, and your approval makes him worse."

"I'm trying to stop him," Shelby said, quietly. "I think if I go to the fool thing I can see how she works it and tell Mr. Crane, and he'll be convinced of her trickery."

"Are you convinced of it?" asked Thorpe.

"I've never seen this one, but it's my opinion all professional mediums are fakes," Shelby replied, seriously; "it may not be so, but I believe I can tell after one investigation. I shall pretend to be greatly impressed and all that, but I'll keep my eyes open. And I'm not going to upset Mr. Crane unnecessarily. But if I think she's just fooling him along for the money that's in it, I'm going to tell him so."

"Even at that," Blair put in, "maybe it's worth the money to him to be fooled. He's rich enough."

"Maybe. But I hate to see a man swindled. However, I've agreed to go with him once, and I'm glad to go. Good-by, I'll report results later."

"You see," Blair said to Thorpe after Shelby had gone, "Kit and I can't help feeling a sort of responsibility for this fad of Mr. Crane's. It may be foolish and sentimental, but we feel an interest in Peter's father, and we watch over him as if Peter had asked us to do so, which, of course, he never did."

"But the medium business is such awful rubbish," objected Thorpe.

"It is and it isn't," Blair said, musingly. "It's six weeks now since we came home, and all that time Mr. Crane has been receiving messages from Peter, and every one of them that I've heard are sane and believable. Moreover, Carlotta Harper has almost convinced me there's something in it. That girl is a sort of medium herself. She denies it, says she only uses her common sense, but I think she's clairvoyant."

"There's a heap of difference between being clairvoyant, in a common sense way, and being a fake medium! I don't care what Miss Harper does with a foolish Ouija Board, but I'm like Kit Shelby, I hate to see Benjamin Crane stung by a wily faker!"

$$*\quad*\quad*\quad*\quad*$$

Meantime Mr. Benjamin Crane was altogether enjoying the process that Thorpe called stinging.

Shelby, deeply interested, and looking innocently credulous, sat by while the medium conducted the *seance*.

Madame Parlato was, as Crane had asserted, a quiet-mannered, refined looking woman, of a gracious and pleasant personality. She was tall and fair, rather English in type, and spoke with a noticeable English accent. She frequently ended sentences of simple statement with a rising inflection and was addicted to the use of the word *very*, which she pronounced *virry*.

"You are a bit skeptical?" she said, with a careless glance at Shelby.

"Only by reason of lack of occasions for belief," he returned. "I am, however, open-minded and fair-minded enough to be willingly convinced. You may or may not know, this son of Mr. Crane's was one of my closest friends, and——"

"Don't advance information, please," she remonstrated, "lest I be thought to make use of it. I will ask you both to be quiet, whilst I compose myself."

"Hush up, Shelby," growled Crane, and Shelby did.

The medium closed her eyes and leaned back in her armchair.

She did not seem to be asleep, but she breathed heavily and a trifle irregularly, and now and then gave a slight convulsive shudder.

At last she spoke, very slowly, and in a voice decidedly different from her own. Shelby couldn't quite make up his mind whether it seemed to him like Peter's voice or not.

The voice said, "I am here, father," and, after a moment's pause, repeated the words.

"Yes, yes," breathed Benjamin Crane, enthralled, as always, by the sound; "talk to me, Peter, tell me things."

"I can't talk much this time, father, it is hard to get through. There is some obstacle."

These words did not follow each other in natural succession, but came haltingly, with waits between. Madame Parlato seemed unconscious of the delays, and merely acted as a mouthpiece for the revelations.

"What sort of an obstacle?" asked Crane.

"An unbeliever is near," the voice hesitatingly asserted.

"Oh, I say!" exclaimed Shelby, "tell him who I am!"

"It's only Shelby," Mr. Crane said, "Kit Shelby. He's not really an unbeliever, only inexperienced."

"May I speak to him?" asked Shelby, as if permission were necessary.

"Go ahead," consented Mr. Crane.

"It's old Kit, Peter—Kit Shelby, who went on the trip with you."

"Oh, Kit—all right—all right, old fellow—can't say much to-night—something wrong——"

"Well, but Peter," Shelby begged, "give me some sort of a sign—a test, you know. I can't help wanting that."

"All right," very slowly, "what test."

"Let me see—well, tell me whose picture you carried in your watch case."

"Why, it was—Caroline—Caroline Harper."

Shelby looked dazed. True, they had never called Carly Caroline, but the Harper was undeniable, and the test quite near enough to the truth.

The medium sat still, save for frequent slight shivers. Suddenly she opened her eyes:

"Who is talking?" she said.

"I am," Shelby told her. "Please let me say a few more things."

Madame Parlato's eyes closed, and she was motionless.

"Are you still there, Peter?" asked his father, who was not at all pleased with the presence of Shelby. It seemed to interfere with the continuous talk he had hitherto enjoyed at the *seances.*

"Yes, father. Is Kit there?"

"Can't you see me, Peter?"

"Not—not clearly. There's a haze in the room."

There was no haze visible to the mortals present, but Shelby went eagerly on.

"Never mind seeing me, Peter, but do tell me this: What happened to you?"

"When?" asked the voice, with a far-away, fading sound.

"When—when you died, you know. Oh, Peter, don't go away until you tell us!"

"Tell you—tell you—what?"

"What killed you? How was it? Did you fall down?"

"I—I fell down, yes."

"In the snowdrifts?"

"Yes, the snow was so cold—"

"But why couldn't you get up? What happened to you? Did any attack——"

"Yes, I was attacked. Attacked by a——"

"What!"

"By a wild animal of some sort."

"Oh, Peter! What was it? Are you sure?"

"No, not sure—but attack by——"

The voice grew fainter and more incoherent, and in a moment the medium sat up straight and shook her head.

"He was troubled," she said, "I could see him though you couldn't, and he was sad and worried."

"What about?" asked Shelby, abruptly.

"I'm not sure, but I think because he didn't want to tell the awful details of his death."

"What were they? Could you see them?"

"Yes," she pushed her loose hair back from her brow, as if exhausted. "Yes, I saw it like a picture, but like a clouded, indistinct picture. The poor chap was fighting a wild beast! Oh, it was fearful!" she shut her eyes and shook her head violently. "That's the worst of it, I see too clearly."

"Tell us more, then," begged Shelby. "How did Peter look?"

"Glorious, transfigured! His face was shining and his eyes sparkling."

"H'm—queer to look like that when he was so worried."

"Oh, that was before the anxious look came. It is, I fear, difficult for you to understand the conditions. The discarnate spirit has a sort of secondary personality, not unlike a hypnotic state, and sometimes this is jarred by any untoward influence and develops into a delirium, and the statements cannot then be relied on. A novice always expects a clear, definite style of speech from a spirit communicating through a medium. This is not always the case. And the medium must merely take what comes and repeat it without change or addition. If, therefore, you are disappointed, I cannot help it. Surely you would not wish me to embroider the messages I receive."

"Surely not," returned Shelby, "indeed, I think it wonderful that you succeeded in getting as much coherence and information as you did. It is something to know that Peter was attacked by a wild beast, for, horrible as is the news, it does explain why he couldn't proceed on the journey."

"Yes," agreed Mr. Crane. "And I am so avid for word from my boy, that even if the messages are disturbing and harrowing, I want them all. I have always told Madame Parlato not to spare me. I prefer to know the worst. For my boy is happy now. We have had several sittings; my wife has attended some, and they are always comforting because of Peter's assertions that he is now happy and contented."

At Shelby's urgent request, the medium endeavored to induce Peter's spirit to return for a further word.

Her success was only partial, but they did hear a message to Shelby direct.

"Persevere, Kit," Peter said, "you're doing right in that matter. Go ahead, Kit."

"Your voice sounds queer, Peter," Shelby said, frowning a little. "It used to be pitched in a higher key."

"It's the medium," came a reply, and the pitch was higher. "I don't mean the human medium, but the medium through which I must talk—the ether, I suppose it is. Good-by, Kit."

Madame Parlato then came out of her trance, or whatever term she used to designate her half-conscious state.

"The session is over," she said, pleasantly. "I fear, Mr. Crane, you did not get your usual degree of satisfaction from it, but that was because of a third party here. I don't think Mr. Shelby's antagonistic exactly, but he's—well, uncertain whether to believe what he hears or not."

"That's quite true, Madame," said Shelby, with due respect, "but you are doubtless accustomed to people in my frame of mind."

"Oh, yes," and the lady smiled a little, "but I trust, Mr. Shelby, you will come some time by yourself and let me see what I can do to help you make up your mind."

"I shall be glad to do that. You have a strange power, at any rate."

"Strange, yes; but by no means unique. There are minds tuned by nature to receive spirit messages, as wireless stations are tuned. I cannot explain my strange power, I marvel at it myself, but I recognize it, and I use it humbly and gratefully as a God-given treasure."

"And that's what it is!" declared Benjamin Crane. "I'm glad you came to-night, Shelby, but, after this, I admit I prefer to come alone, or with only my wife. The messages from Peter to his father are naturally more of a loving and domestic nature, and I revel in them."

"I don't wonder at that, Mr. Crane. And I congratulate you on having found such a capable and skillful medium."

Madame Parlato gave Shelby a quick glance, almost as if doubting his sincerity. But his frank, honest face reassured her, and she said:

"And, I'm proud to say, I'm not only a medium, but I am possessed of the power that is called impersonation or transfiguration. This is comparatively rare, and it enables me to perform what really seem like miracles. I am taken possession of by the departed subject, and I speak and act so perfectly with that other personality that sometimes I even resemble the person who is talking through me."

"It is indeed wonderful," Shelby said, and Benjamin Crane looked happily contemplative of the *seances* in the future when Madame would utilize this miraculous gift of hers in his behalf.

*   *   *   *   *

Shelby did go alone to see the medium, and it happened also that, about a week later, going again, he chanced to meet Mr. Crane there. The younger man offered to leave, but Crane said, "No, come along. Madame is going to try to-night to materialize Peter's face, and I want you here to see it."

And so the strange *seance* began.

Materialization, of course, called for a darkened room, and Shelby's naturally suspicious mind was alert for possible fraud.

But he could discover no chance for such. There was no cabinet, no tambourine, bell or trumpet, and no curtain was drawn or screen set up.

After they had sat in darkness and silence for a time, a face seemed to form in mid-air. It was a misty, vague countenance, and was wrapped about with a soft, floating drapery or veil, which exposed only the features.

"Peter!" exclaimed Benjamin Crane in a half-gasping voice. "My boy himself!"

"Peter Boots!" cried Shelby, and slowly the face vanished.

Not another word was spoken, and in a moment the lights were turned on. This was done by Madame Parlato, at whose elbow the light switch was.

"Did you see anything?" she asked, in an exhausted, harassed way, yet with an air of eagerness.

"Yes," cried out Crane. "I saw Peter, my own son!"

"I couldn't be sure," she went on, speaking wearily. "It always exhausts me utterly to induce a materialization, and I doubt if I can achieve anything more to-night."

"Nor do you need to," declared Mr. Crane. "That's enough for one *seance*. Some time you may do that again, and also get speech from him."

"May be," she rejoined, with a gentle politeness, "and now I should be glad to say good-night."

The two men walked off, Crane in a tumult of delight, Shelby wondering at it all.

"You accept marvels very easily, Mr. Crane," the latter said.

"Because they are marvels," said the older man simply. "If they were fraud it would be no marvel. But being genuine, it is a marvel, it is a miracle, and I am glad, rejoiced to accept it!"

*   *   *   *   *

It was soon after this that Shelby, calling on Carlotta Harper, asked her what she thought of it all.

"Rubbish," she replied flatly.

Shelby looked at her. "But," he said, "I've been told that you can work the Ouija Board wonderfully!"

"Work the Ouija Board! What sort of talk is that? Do you mean push it, to spell what I want it to?"

"No; I spoke carelessly. I mean use the Board with results that are surprising."

"Who can't do that?"

"Lots of people—myself, for one. Let's try it now, Carly. Will you?"

"Certainly, if you like. And, if you'll give me your word of honor that you won't voluntarily or purposely urge the thing in any direction or toward any letter."

"Of course I promise that! Where'd be the fun if we cheated? You promise, too?"

"Yes, indeed. Like you, I've no interest if either pushes the least mite."

They placed themselves with the board between them on their knees.

It was but a short time before the little heart-shaped block began to move.

Carly, who was no novice, said in a sing-song way: "Is there a spirit present?"

The board slid quickly to the corner marked "yes."

"Will you spell out your name?" Carly went on in a very matter-of-fact voice.

The pointer went from letter to letter, now hurriedly and now making wide circling sweeps, but it spelled correctly "Peter Boots."

Shelby kept most careful watch on Carly's finger-tips. He could see that there was no apparent muscle movement, no surreptitious pushing and no motion of any sort save to follow the moving board. Her hands were quite evidently resting as lightly as his own on the wood, and the board without doubt moved without the voluntary help of either.

"Shall we go on?" asked Carly, in a half whisper.

"Go on? Of course!" returned the other.

"Peter, have you a message for us?" Carly asked, again using that calm, uninflected tone.

"Yes," pointed the board, and then, as they settled down to receive it, the wooden heart spelled rapidly: "Do not grieve for me— I am happy."

Carlotta looked disappointed. "Oh, dear," she said, "I'm so tired of that message! I thought Peter would do better than that! Let's try again."

Again the board moved, and the message came, "Tell mother not to grieve——"

"Oh, Peter," Carlotta said, in real impatience, "do say something beside those stereotyped phrases! Tell us something we don't know, something about yourself."

"Tell us how you died," said Shelby, suddenly.

"Yes, tell us that," Carly repeated.

The board moved more slowly.

"I was," it spelled, and "Go on!" the girl urged "I was— in the snow——"

"Yes, yes—go on."

"And I fell down, and I—I—couldn't get up."

"Why not?" this sharply from Carly.

"H——" the board stopped; then went on, "Heart failure."

"I thought so!" exclaimed Shelby; "there aren't any wild animals up there in——"

"Hush—it's moving again," said Carly.

"Heart gave out," the board spelled, moving rapidly now. "Couldn't make the boys hear. Could only gurgle in my throat. Couldn't shout. So I died."

"Do you believe it?" asked Carly, her big, brown eyes solemn and serious.

"Yes, I do," said Shelby. "It's highly probable, anyway. Go on, Peter, tell us something else."

Whether Shelby "believed" or not, he was deeply interested, and his breath came faster as he saw the revealing letters spell various messages.

Both performers watched the four hands as the board moved under them. And, the most intense scrutiny could discover no voluntary movement or assistance to the uncanny instrument.

Many messages were of slight importance, and then came a sudden, "I say, Shelby, why don't you marry Carly?"

The girl gasped, then smiled, but Shelby looked up, dumbfounded.

"Oh, Carly," he said, "if you only would!"

"Hush!" she reproved him. "I'll put the board away if you do such things! You know you pushed it that time!"

"I didn't, Carly, truly—word of honor, I didn't! I'd no idea what was coming! Oh, Carly, darling, I love you, and—dear, whether Peter sent that message or not—won't you—can't you——"

They had risen, casting aside the board, and Shelby took her hands in his. "Dearest," he said, "I wanted to tell you, but I was waiting—for—for Peter's sake. Now—he wants it! So, dear heart—my little girl—won't you——"

"No," said Carlotta.

CHAPTER 7: THE TOBACCO POUCH

It was doubtless owing to Benjamin Crane's attitude regarding his son's death that the home did not present more the aspect of a house of mourning. Both Crane and his wife were not only resigned to Peter's fate, but they seemed positively happy in what they believed to be continued communion with his spirit.

As Mrs. Crane said, "When Peter was a child the gypsies said he would go away and be lost, but he would return to us. He has done so, he is doing so—why should we grieve? He tells us he is happy and contented in his new sphere of existence, therefore, we are, too."

"That's all very well," Carlotta Harper would respond, "but I don't look at it that way at all. I want my Peter Boots back again in the flesh. I'm not contented at all with a lot of spirit talk communicated through a paid medium!"

"Don't say paid medium, as if the paying detracted from her worth," Benjamin Crane chid the girl. "Of course, we pay Madame Parlato for her time—why should we not? It's the best money I ever spent! And you're a medium yourself, Carlotta. You hate to acknowledge it, but you are. Your work with the Ouija Board is perfectly marvelous, and I have proved to my own satisfaction that you never use the least fraud."

"Indeed, I don't," said Carlotta, earnestly, "but what's the use? What do I care to have Peter talk on that wooden board—if it *is* Peter—I want him, himself!"

Carlotta was passing through strange moods. Living alone with her mother, their home seemed far more a house of mourning than the Cranes'.

The girl grieved deeply for Peter. Though not definitely engaged, she knew their betrothal would have

been sealed on his return. And not having the comfort
that the Cranes so gladly accepted, she sorrowed for her
lost love.

Her success with the Ouija Board was a matter of
mystery to her mother and to all who knew of it. It
seemed that she must be a medium, or possess some
occult power, for whenever she placed her finger-tips on
the little board it immediately began to move, and told
such remarkable things that there was occasion for
surprise. Nor did Carlotta move the board of her own
volition. It was easily seen that she did not "push" or urge
it in any direction. The most careful scrutiny could not
only discern no effort of hers, but could not fail to be
convinced that she made none. Her friends came often to
beg her to give them a session. Her fame spread until it
began to annoy her.

Gilbert Blair talked to her about it.

"You know, Carly," he said, "it's not really a message
from a spirit you get, it's——"

"It's what, Gilbert?" she asked, smiling. "Don't you tell
me it's fraud on my part, because it isn't."

"No, I don't think it's conscious fraud, but——"

"But you don't know what it is, do you?" the girl
smiled at him, and Blair, looking deep in her eyes, said:
"No, I don't know what it is, and I don't care. But I care
about you. Carly, dear, can't you learn to love me? I'm not
as good a chap as Peter—dear old Peter. But I love you—
oh, girl, how I love you!"

"The Ouija Board said that Peter wanted me to turn
my affections toward Kit Shelby."

"It didn't! did it? Then that proves that it was no real
message from Peter! He would rather you'd turn toward
me."

"How do you know?"

"Oh, we used to talk about you up in the snows of
Labrador. And Peter loved you lots, but he knew I did,
too, and we agreed that the best man should win. I don't

mean the best man, but the one who stood best in your heart. And now—oh, Carly, if you only would——"

"Not yet, Gilbert—don't let's talk about it yet."

"But Peter's been dead nearly six months, and you weren't actually engaged, you know——"

"How do you know that?"

"Peter told me, oh, we were confidential up there. And, now, Peter's gone, and try, won't you, Carly, try to love me. Shelby isn't in my way, is he?"

"I don't know—he wants to be."

"Of course he does! But I won't give up to him! Peter was different. He was a wonder, that chap!"

"Indeed, he was. And I care too much for his memory to think about any one else—yet."

"But some day, Carly—dear, some day?"

"Some day we'll see about it. Gilbert, what do you think of that medium the Cranes go to all the time?"

"Absolute rubbish."

"I think that, too. But she's doing queer stunts. She's begun materializing things."

"What sort of things?"

"I don't know exactly. Flowers, I believe, and hands and faces."

"You know all the legerdemain people do that."

"That's no argument, Gilbert, and you know it. The charlatans can do all the things that the real mediums do. The question is not whether the fakers can do them, but whether the real mediums can."

"Meaning whether the real mediums are real or not?"

"Yes, that's what I mean. If ever there was a real one. I think Madame Parlato is one. But I'm not sure. She does the Cranes a lot of good. They believe——"

"Not Julie."

"Oh, no, Julie hates the whole business. I think she'd be convinced, though, except for Mr. Thorpe. He's such a skeptic that he influences Julie."

"I *thought* Thorpe was rather interested in that direction."

"Well, rather! Why, they've been exclusively interested in each other all winter."

"Thorpe's a close-mouthed chap. We live together, but we seldom exchange confidences. I like him pretty well, but——"

"But what?"

"I oughtn't to say it, but I don't altogether trust him. We're working for a prize, you know, the Callender medal, and sometimes I've imagined that he——"

"I know, he steals your ideas."

"Well, I wouldn't put it so bluntly, but he is an unconscious kleptomaniac, I think. He watches my drawing—I go astray sometimes to mislead him—and next thing I know he incorporates the same motive in his own sketches. I wouldn't say this to any one else, but I'm a little worried about it. Not so much about his taking my stuff as the fear that some one will think I've taken his."

"How's your work progressing?"

"Well—if Thorpe lets me alone."

"Can't you lock yourself in?"

"Oh, no; we use the same studio, and if I seemed fearful he would be angry at once. He's a strange nature, Thorpe. Morbid and secretive, yet a good friend and a first-rate living companion. You see, we've separate bedrooms, of course, but we've only the one big room that's studio and sitting-room combined. We have to use it together, but as our friends are pretty much the same bunch, we get along all right. We have lockers and all that, but I hate to lock up my sketches when I go out. It looks as if I didn't trust him."

"Well, you don't."

"No; but I can't tell him so. Nor do I want to hint it— at least not until I find some definite proof. Get out your Ouija Board, Carly, and see if it will tell us anything."

"Oho, you believe in it fast enough when you want to use it?"

But a trial of the occult only brought Blair the advice to beware of a friend who might be at heart an enemy. To be careful of his plans and sketches, for there was some one near who might be guilty of deceit.

All of which Blair knew before.

*   *   *   *   *

The sessions which the Cranes held with Madame Parlato increased in importance and interest.

She had succeeded in materializing the face and form of their son to their satisfaction of his identity. They told remarkable tales of seeing and hearing Peter Boots, until Julie ran out of the room lest she voice her disapproval too strongly. For Julie Crane, though an absolute unbeliever in Madame Parlato and all her works, was a devoted daughter, and would do nothing to disturb the happiness her parents felt in the *seances* with the medium.

But one performance fairly staggered the group of listeners to whom the Cranes recounted it.

They returned from the medium's to find the young people sitting round the hospitable Crane fireside. It was mid March and the weather still allowed of the cheerful open fire.

Carlotta was there and Shelby, and Blair and Thorpe, with Julie, of course, made up the little party.

"The most marvelous yet!" Benjamin Crane exclaimed, as he drew near the fire. "Julie, dear, if you don't want to hear, run away, for I must tell about it."

But Julie stayed, and her parents told the story.

It seemed the medium had promised them something very definite by way of proof, and she had certainly kept her promise.

The materialization of Peter had taken place, and, as the spirit form slowly dissolved and faded from their view, there was left behind, lying on the table, an object that had not been there before.

It was a tobacco pouch, old and worn, and bearing Peter's initials.

Julie looked at it with horror-stricken eyes, as her father produced it from his pocket.

"Why," she gasped, "it's the one I gave him on his birthday."

"Not really!" cried Shelby, and both he and Blair leaned eagerly forward to look.

"It's the one he always carried with him in Labrador," Blair said, with an expression of blank wonderment. "How did it get down here?"

"I offer no explanation, save the true one," Benjamin Crane said, seriously. "That is, as you see, a real object. It is Peter's property. You, Blair, recognize it. Do you, Shelby?"

"I do," Shelby replied, his eyes staring at the thing.

"Julie recognized it at once," went on Crane. "So there's no doubt of its identity. Now, I submit that it would be impossible for Madame Parlato to have come by this in any natural way, therefore it is supernatural."

"Supernatural!" McClellan Thorpe exclaimed, with utter scorn in his voice. "How could that be, sir?"

"It was materialized by my son, Peter," Crane returned, looking at Thorpe, calmly. "That may seem incredible to you, but it is not so incredible as any other explanation you may offer. You cannot think my wife or I would misstate what happened, can you? You cannot assume that Madame Parlato obtained this in any underhanded way, for you cannot conceive of any way in which she *could* do so. Then, what do you suggest?"

"Anything, but that Peter brought it!" Thorpe cried.

"Ah, yes; anything but the truth. You glibly say 'anything,' but I ask you to suggest what you mean in that 'anything,' and you fail to reply."

"There is nothing to suggest," Blair said; "I confess myself utterly at a loss to suggest anything. To my certain knowledge Peter had that on his person when he died! Why, that morning he had given me a pipeful out of it, and had then returned it to his pocket! My explanation is that Peter is alive!"

"I wish that were the true one," said Benjamin Crane, fervently, "but if you'll think a minute, Gilbert, you'll realize that if Peter were alive he would come to us in the flesh, and not send his tobacco pouch by a medium."

"Indeed, he would!" agreed Carlotta, "much as I'd love to believe Peter alive, this episode contradicts such a belief, not proves it!"

"That's right," said Shelby, thoughtfully; "I, too, can believe anything rather than that the medium caused the materialization of this thing, but——"

"The medium didn't cause it, exactly," broke in Mrs. Crane's gentle voice; "you see, we had begged Peter so hard for a material proof that he promised to try to give it to us. And at last he succeeded. It is miraculous, of course, but no more miraculous than the strange things recorded in the Bible. You see, I hold that the day of miracles is not past."

Shelby said gravely, "You must be right, for there's surely no other explanation. I, too, saw this in Peter's hand that last day we were together. I can't believe he's alive——"

"Of course not!" interrupted Blair, "if he were, he'd have no use for mediums! Whatever is the truth, it's not that Peter's alive! I only wish it might be, but as Carlotta says, this thing contradicts such a theory. I'm beaten. I see no light at all."

Benjamin Crane smiled. "You boys admit you see no explanation yet you refuse to accept the obvious and only one possible. But I'm not going to try to persuade you, I've no reason to do so. It all means little to you, but it is as the breath of life to me and to Peter's mother. I trust that some day Julie will be convinced of these truths, but that is for her to decide. I shall add this revelation to my book, by way of an appendix. It's too late to incorporate it in the body of the work."

Benjamin Crane's book had been a work of absorbing interest to him if not to his friends. He was entirely obsessed by the whole matter of Spiritism, and his book, following the style of a celebrated work of a similar nature in England, was even now in the publisher's hands.

The book was a memorial to Peter and an account of the experiences of his parents during the sessions with the medium. Crane possessed a pleasant, convincing style, and the book was well written and of a real interest quite apart from the question of the reader's belief in its matter.

*   *   *   *   *

When the volume was published, and that was early in April, it became an immediate success. Not the least of the reasons for this was the astounding account of the materialization of the tobacco pouch, detailed exactly as Benjamin Crane had told the story the night of the occurrence.

The book went like wildfire. Edition after edition was sold, and Benjamin Crane found himself famous. The benign old gentleman took his notoriety calmly, and refused to see the people who thronged to his door unless they were personal acquaintances. He had to engage secretaries and other assistants, but his methodical and efficient mind easily coped with all such matters. Mrs. Crane, too, was serenely indifferent to the publicity of it all, and pursued her simple ways of life undisturbed.

But Julie was angry at it all. Her life, she said, was spoiled by being known as the daughter of a demented monomaniac.

Her father smiled at her and told her she would change her views some day, and her mother scolded her now and then, but mostly ignored the subject when talking with her.

Julie found sympathy in the views of McClellan Thorpe.

Neither of these two would believe in the materialization of the tobacco pouch, yet neither of them could arrive at any satisfactory explanation of the incident.

"Of course, it's Peter's pouch," Julie would say; "but it came to that woman by some natural means. Maybe, somebody found it up there in Labrador and brought it home——"

"No," Thorpe would object, "in that case it would be weather-worn and defaced, and, too, nobody would have any reason to find it, bring it home, and give it to Madame Parlato! No, Carly, that won't do."

"Maybe he had two—duplicates," Carly suggested once. But inquiries of the Crane family proved that was not so. It was the very one Julie had given her brother, she was sure of that.

And so that mystery remained unexplained, save by the acceptance of a miracle.

A very material result of the success of Crane's book was a large amount of money that came to him from its royalties. Some of this he decided to use in fitting out an expedition to recover his son's body.

This, he decreed, was to be under the direction of Shelby and Blair, who knew just how it should be conducted. With his usual efficiency, Crane made all the arrangements and then told the young men about what he had done.

They agreed to go, but Shelby advised first that he write to Joshua, their old guide, as to their reception.

This was done, but the reply received caused a halt in the preparations.

For the letter, which Shelby brought over for Crane to read, ran thus:

"DEAR MISTER SHELBY:

"I think youd better not try to take back the boddy of Mister Peter. We berried it verry deep and it better remain here. Anny way, you cant mannage it till late summer. Say about August or so."

"However, Mr. Crane," Shelby said, "if you say so, we can go ahead in spite of Joshua's letter. He's a good guide, but he always was a bit dictatorial."

"No," Benjamin Crane said, "I believe in taking advice from one who is undoubtedly good authority. We'll postpone the plan until August."

When Blair was told of it he was rather relieved, for he was busy with his prize drawings and he didn't want to leave town.

"Let's see the letter," he said to Shelby.

"I haven't it, Blair. I left it with Mr. Crane. But I've told you the gist of it."

"All right, Kit," and Blair went on with his work.

It was the next night at the Crane house that Mr. Crane again spoke of his disappointment at not putting through his hoped-for expedition.

"You see, Kit," he said to Shelby, "I want to write another book, and I want it to be about the recovery of Peter's body."

"Oh, don't do that, Mr. Crane," Shelby said, impulsively; "it would be anti-climax. You've done a big thing, and scored a success. Another book would spoil it all."

"I don't think so," said Crane, not at all annoyed at Shelby's attitude. "Anyway, I hate to give up my plan. See here, Shelby, are you sure that man Joshua wrote the letter you got?"

"Why, yes. What makes you ask that?"

"Only because it's in a big sprawly hand, and once Blair showed me a letter from Joshua, which he's kept as a memento, and it was in a small cramped hand."

"That's queer. But I expect Joshua might have got somebody to write for him. Those half-breeds are not very scholarly, you know. However, if there's any doubt about it, the matter must be looked into. Do you mean that maybe we can go now, after all? But I can't help thinking that Joshua wrote that. I know he's not very strong on spelling!"

"Well, Blair will know. You ask him for that letter he has of Joshua's."

"All right, Mr. Crane, I will. I'll see him to-night. There's a dinner on at the Club, and he'll be there. You know he's in a fair way, I think, to get that Callender prize."

"I hope so, I'm sure. A rising young architect, Blair is, and I hope he wins it. I suppose he wouldn't want to go to Labrador until that matter is settled?"

"No, probably not. But the award will be made this month."

"And he's in a fair way to get it?"

"Looks that way to me. His sketches are fine, though I haven't seen his finished work. Thorpe's a close second, I imagine."

"I suppose I'd rather see Thorpe get it, but don't tell Blair that. A man is naturally interested in his future son-in-law."

"Oh, it's gone as far as that, has it?"

"Yes, but it's not announced yet. So say nothing till Julie tells you to. She's a dear girl, but as hard as adamant where belief in the occult is concerned."

"She and Thorpe are at one there."

"Yes, that helped the affair along, I fancy. But it's all right. Julie can think what she likes. Peter used to hate the subject, too."

"I know it. We touched on it now and then, but he usually veered off to something else at once."

"What do you think about the pouch, Shelby? I'm not sure I ever asked you."

"I don't think, Mr. Crane. I mean I can't explain the thing by natural means, and I'm unable to believe in the supernatural. What more can I say?"

"Nothing. I suppose most people are like that. Thank heaven. I'm made so that I can believe!"

Chapter 8: Blair Knows

Gilbert Blair was a lovable sort of chap, one of those fine, gentle natures that will put up with annoyance rather than annoy another. Although he would have preferred to live alone, yet it was greatly to his pecuniary advantage to have Thorpe share his place, and, on the whole, they got on fairly well. But, being of different habits and temperaments, the details of their home life were not always harmonious.

Blair was methodical, liked his drawing implements and sketches kept in order, and the rooms tidy. Thorpe was not particular in these respects, and his belongings were always scattered about not only on his own tables or desk, but on Blair's. Moreover, he did not hesitate to use his chum's materials if his own were not immediately available.

So it happened that when Shelby stopped in on his way home from the Cranes' he found a mild war of words in progress.

"You know, old dear," Thorpe was saying, "you'd be quite welcome to use my drawing paper, and I call it rough of you to kick because I took a couple of sheets of yours."

"Couple of sheets!" exclaimed Blair, "you took six or eight, and I had only about enough to complete this series of sketches. You know how I hate to use paper that doesn't match——"

"At it again?" said Shelby, coming in. "You two never have an out and out row, but you're always bickering. Thorpe, you ought to mend your ways—it is a confounded nuisance to have other people using your things."

"Oh, Blair's an old granny. It does him good to get stirred up once in a while. That paper of his——"

"I know," said Shelby, quietly, "it's a special paper that he bought for his prize drawings—it's not only expensive, but he wants the sheets uniform. You knew this, Thorpe, and yet you grab it and use it for your trial sketches."

"Now, now, Kit," and Blair smiled good-naturedly, "you needn't take up my quarrel. I'm jumping on Thorpe myself."

"You jumping! You'd lie down and let him walk over you!"

"Not much, he wouldn't!" Thorpe growled; "he's been ballyragging me for half an hour! Not only about the paper, but he——"

"Let up, Thorpe," Blair spoke angrily, "at least let's keep our skeletons in our closet!"

"Oh, is there a real row on?" Shelby inquired.

"No, no," Blair declared, but Thorpe jumped up, and, going into his bedroom, closed the door behind him.

"Drop it," commanded Blair, quietly, and Shelby changed the subject.

"Mr. Crane says you had an old letter from Joshua," he began, "let's see it, will you?"

"Sure, if I can find it," and Blair began rummaging in his desk. "Confound it, Kit, if Thorpe hasn't been poking in here among my letters!"

"I wouldn't stand for it, Gilbert. What would he do that for?"

"Hush," with a glance toward Thorpe's closed door, "never mind now. But, anyway, I can't find that letter. What do you want it for?"

"Mr. Crane thinks the one I received from Joshua looks so different that I wanted to compare them."

"Let me see yours. I can tell at once. Joshua wrote a small cramped hand——"

"This one was rather large and of loosely formed letters, but, of course, some one may have written it for him."

"Yes, Joshua hated to write——"

"Well, never mind, don't hunt for it any more. Pretty queer thing about that tobacco pouch of Peter's, don't you think?"

Blair looked up quickly. "No, I don't. I know, or at least I think I know, the explanation of that."

"You do! Well, out with it!"

"No, not now," and Blair gave a significant glance toward Thorpe's door. "But I've had my suspicions roused, and I'm going to verify them, and then I'm going to expose somebody. I can't stand any more of this sort of thing. I tell you, Kit, I know!"

Shelby looked at him in amazement.

"Well, if you won't talk now, we'll whoop it up some other time. See you to-night at the dinner?"

"Yes; get along now, and we'll meet there later."

Blair looked anxious and preoccupied. As he went toward the door with Shelby he said suddenly, "I say, Kit, will you drop Carlotta Harper?"

"Drop her!"

"Yes; stop calling on her or paying her any attention."

"I will not! Just why——"

"All right." Blair's voice was cold and sharp. "Good night."

"Good night, Gil. You're queer to-night. See you later."

*   *   *   *   *

While dressing for the dinner Kit Shelby thought long and earnestly of Blair's strange words and his peculiar mental attitude. He thought Blair was like a man who had reached the end of his rope. A sort of exasperation had showed in his face and manner, and Shelby wondered what it meant.

He went over every word of the conversation they had had, including Blair's demand that Shelby desist from future acquaintance with Carly Harper! That was some demand, Shelby decided. And one to which he had no intention of acceding.

His ruminations resulted in his calling again at Blair's on the way to the dinner.

He found Blair nearly ready, and Thorpe, too, waiting to start.

Shelby scrutinized the faces of both men, and concluded they were still at odds. He went into Blair's bedroom, where that correct young man was carefully tying his immaculate evening tie.

"There, you made me spoil it," Blair exclaimed, as Shelby's sudden entrance caused a nervous gesture and a resultant wrinkle of the strip of lawn.

"Fiddle-de-dee! Don't be a fuss! Only men, you know. That's good enough."

But Blair selected another tie, and, while he manipulated it, Shelby fussed around the room. He could say no word in confidence to Blair, for Thorpe was impatiently tailing them to hurry, and shortly the three started off, gay of manner on the surface, whatever they might be thinking about.

They carefully avoided all mention of the Cranes, and also avoided the coming prize competition as a subject of discussion.

This, itself, proved the rift in the lute was still recognized in the souls of Blair and Thorpe at least. The two had enough artistic temperament to feel the inevitable jealousy of each other's designs, and if Blair suspected Thorpe of appropriating his ideas, whether consciously or unintentionally, it would have the effect of making him unusually quiet, even morose, rather than to result in so much as a spoken hint of his thoughts.

Moreover, habit is strong, and the three walked off to keep their engagement with much the same gay laughter and chatter as usual.

Shelby, especially, was purposely talkative and jocular, for he wanted to get the other two in complete good humor before the feast began.

In a general way he succeeded, and though Blair was a bit quiet, Thorpe regained his ordinary temper, and the men met and mingled with their fellows, their attitude properly in the key of the occasion.

It was a merry little dinner, and at last the talk drifted to Mr. Crane's book about Peter. Everybody present had known and loved Peter Boots, and various were the opinions regarding Benjamin Crane's extraordinary work.

"All rubbish," declared one man. "Strange, how sensible men can fall for that stuff! Makes me sick!"

"Oh, come now," another urged, "there must be something in it. Benjamin Crane never made up all that."

"No, he didn't make it up, but he was fooled, gulled, taken in."

"By the medium?" asked some one.

"Partly," answered somebody else. "But I think there's been underhand work going on."

"Such as what?"

"Oh, some of Peter's people or friends helping the medium along. I've read that book with the greatest care, studied it, and I get a lot between the lines. And I think——"

"Don't say it," put in Blair, quietly. "Unless you know something, Knight, better keep still."

"But why, Blair? We're all friends of Peter here, why not discuss the thing freely and frankly?"

"Better let it alone," insisted Blair, and then the talk drifted to the coming competition, which was even more dangerous.

"Of course nobody has a look-in but Blair and Thorpe," declared the talkative Knight. "They're sure to get the prize, separately or together."

"What do you mean by that?"

"Heard you were working on a big scheme on which you had joined forces."

"Nothing of the sort," declared Blair, shortly, and Thorpe added, "And if we were, we wouldn't say so."

Then the more peaceable minded of the group
introduced other subjects, and art and spiritism were left
out of it.

*   *   *   *   *

On the way home, as several were walking together,
Shelby turned off at his home street and refused all
invitations to go on with the others.

"Can't do it," he said. "I've got a piece of work to
finish, and I've got to go home. See you all to-morrow
night. By-by."

"I'm going along with you," Knight said to Blair. "I
want to see your sketches, you said I might."

"All right," Gilbert returned, and, Thorpe with them,
they went on to the studio.

Knight acted as a peacemaker, though not knowing it.
He was a jolly, good-natured man, and he guyed the work
of both his friends until they joined forces to contradict
him.

Late they sat, smoking and talking over general
matters. Also they discussed the Crane book, and agreed
that, whether true or not, it was a great document and
wonderfully popular.

"People are crazy over it, who always hooted at that
sort of thing," Knight asserted. "It's partly the charm of
Mr. Crane's manner, for the book is delightfully written,
and somehow it does carry conviction."

"Thought you didn't believe in it!"

"Me? Oh, I don't," and Knight winked; "I mean it
carries conviction to those who like that sort of thing. No,
I don't believe a word of it is truth."

"Yet you have confidence in Mr. Crane's sincerity?"

"Oh, yes; he's merely fooled by a medium and——"

"Go on."

"And somebody who's telling her things."

"Who'd do that?"

"I don't know, but it's too palpable. Look at that tobacco pouch affair. You know somebody must have given her that. Who did?"

"Hush up," said Blair, determinedly. "If you want to discuss that, do it somewhere else."

"You're all on edge to-night, Blairsy. What's the matter?"

"Nothing, and I'm not."

"Oh, yes, you are," Knight went on. "But, of course, it's nervousness about the competition. What'll either of you boys do if the other gets the prize?"

"Congratulate him," said Thorpe, but there was not much ring of earnestness in his tone.

Blair looked at him moodily, and Knight rose to go.

"You chaps are out of sorts, and I'll not see you again till the prize business is settled. Then I hope you'll be your own sweet sunny selves once more. Good night."

He went off, and the other two began a desultory conversation. It lagged, however, and soon they separated for the night.

* * * * *

Nobody in the Leonardo Studio apartments was an early riser. For that reason it was nearly eleven o'clock when Thorpe, his face very white, telephoned downstairs and asked the doorman to come up at once.

When Hastings appeared he found Thorpe sitting on the edge of a chair in the studio in a state of agitation.

"Blair——" Thorpe said, speaking with difficulty. "Mr. Blair,—you know,—he's—he's very ill——"

"Ill, sir? Where is he?"

"In bed—in his room—go in, Hastings."

The man went in, and it needed only a glance to tell him that Blair's illness, whatever it had been, was fatal.

"He's dead," Hastings said, in an awe-stricken voice. "He's surely dead."

"Well, do something," Thorpe said; "what's the thing to do? Get a doctor?"

"A doctor couldn't help him, but yes, we ought to send for one. Who, sir?"

"I don't know. I've never had a doctor. This unnerves me, Hastings. I wish you'd do what's necessary."

"Ain't you a friend of his, sir? Can't you show a little heart?"

Hastings had never liked Thorpe, but had always been an admirer of Gilbert Blair. There was no special reason for this, unless that Blair was of a kindlier nature, and rarely found fault with Hastings, while Thorpe was sometimes irascible and even unreasonable.

Moreover, if Thorpe was nervously upset, Hastings was, too, and neither man knew exactly what to do.

"Well, you must get a doctor," Thorpe went on, a little peevishly. "You're responsible in cases of emergency——"

"Me responsible, sir? What do you mean, Mr. Thorpe?"

"Nothing to make you look like that. But you're in a position of responsibility, and it's up to you to do something. Now, do it."

"Yes, sir." The tone of authority brought Hastings to his senses. He was responsible in a case like this, and he went to the telephone. He called the superintendent, who did not live in the building, and asked him to come at once, and to bring a doctor. Then, his work done, he left the room, and Thorpe was alone with his dead comrade.

But McClellan Thorpe made no move. He sat still on the edge of the chair, his face turned away from Blair's bedroom and toward the outer door.

At last Somers, the superintendent, arrived, and with him was Doctor Frost.

They went straight to Blair's bedroom, scarcely speaking to Thorpe.

"Hastings tells me he's dead," Somers merely said, as he passed Thorpe's chair.

With practiced experience, the doctor examined the body.

"The man has been dead about eight or nine hours," he said, "it's impossible to fix the time of his death exactly,—but I place it at about three o'clock this morning. Though it may have taken place an hour sooner or later."

"What caused it?" Somers, asked, "a stroke?"

"Can't tell without an autopsy. There is positively no indication of any reason for it."

"A natural death, of course?" Thorpe asked, jerkily.

The doctor gave him a quick glance. "Looks so," he returned. "Maybe a stroke,—though he's young for that. Maybe acute indigestion, is he troubled that way?"

"With indigestion? Yes," Thorpe said; "he has it most of the time. But not acute,—merely a little discomfort when he overeats,—which he often does."

"Does he take anything for it?"

"I don't know,—yes, I've seen him take remedies now and then. I've not paid it much attention."

"Queer case," the doctor mused. "If it had been that, he would have cried out, I think. Did you hear no disturbance?"

"Not a bit," said Thorpe. "Are you sure it's not a stroke?"

"He's too young for a stroke. Where are his people?"

"'Way out West. And he hasn't many. An invalid mother, and a young sister,— I think that's all."

"Well,—who should be notified? Those relatives? Where are they? Will you take charge?"

"Oh, I can't!" Thorpe spoke shrinkingly. "I'm— I'm no relation,—you know,—merely a fellow lodger in his apartment. I'd—rather get out, any way."

"You and he chums?"

"Yes; both architects. Of course, I know all about Mr. Blair's work and that,—but I know nothing of his private affairs. Can't you get somebody to—to settle up his estate?"

"If he has an estate to settle. But somebody ought to look after things. Who are his friends?"

"Mr. Crane is one,—Benjamin Crane. And Christopher Shelby,—he's an intimate chum."

"Crane, the man who wrote the book about his son's spirit?"

"Yes, that one. Shall I telephone him?"

"Yes; you'd better do so. And I think it necessary to have an autopsy. This death is mysterious, to say the least. It's unusual, too, in some of its aspects."

"Do what you like," said Thorpe, "but—but I'd rather not be present. I think I'll go down to the Cranes' and tell them,—while you—you go on with your work."

"All right," said Doctor Frost, "I'd just as lief have you out of the way. Leave me the telephone call that will reach you."

*   *   *   *   *

As Thorpe went off, he realized that he'd had no breakfast. He felt little like eating, but dropped into a restaurant for a cup of coffee.

He found himself totally unable to drink it, and leaving it untasted he went on to the Crane house.

He told the story to Benjamin Crane, who was shocked indeed.

"But I'm not greatly surprised," Mr. Crane said; "I've been thinking for some time that Blair didn't look well. A sort of pallor, you know, and he was thin. I don't think the Labrador trip agreed with him at all. And Peter's death affected him deeply. No; Blair hasn't been well for months."

"What are you doing here at this time in the morning, McClellan?" asked a laughing voice, as Julie Crane came into the room.

But her laughter was hushed as she was told the news.

"Oh, Mac, what an awful ordeal for you," she exclaimed, her sorrow at Blair's death apparently lost sight of in sympathy for Thorpe.

"It was, Julie," he returned, earnestly; "I'm—I'm positively foolish about such things,—death, I mean. I,—I almost went all to pieces."

"Of course you did! Had you had your breakfast?"

"No; I tried to take some coffee, but I couldn't."

"You will now," said the girl, decidedly. "You come with me, to the dining room, and I'll make you some coffee myself, on the electric percolator, and some toast, too, and if you don't enjoy them, I'll be mad at you."

He followed her in a sort of daze, turning back to say: "Are you going up to the studio, Mr. Crane?"

"Yes, at once. You go along with Julie, and let her look after you. And, Julie, you must tell your mother. It will be a shock,—she loves all Peter's friends."

The two went to the dining-room, where Julie, housewifely girl that she was, brewed golden coffee and made toast with no aid from the servants.

Mrs. Crane joined them, and Julie told her mother the sad news.

"Poor Gilbert," she said, wiping her tears away. "Peter loved him. Have you told Kit Shelby?"

"Not yet," Thorpe said; "I'm so broken up myself——"

"Of course you are," Julie said; "I suppose father will send him word. Don't think about that, Mac, father will attend to everything."

"I know it," said Thorpe, "and I'm so relieved. Don't think me a weakling, but death always unnerves me,—I can't help it,—and when I found Gilbert,—like that——"

"There, there," Julie soothed him, "you did all you could. Now let me make you one little piece more of brown toast——"

But Thorpe declined. To please the girl he managed to eat one tiny crisp bit, but another he could not accept. Nor could he take more than a small part of the cup of coffee she gave him.

"I'm a fool," he said, "but—I'm all in!"

CHAPTER 9: INVESTIGATION

Nor did Thorpe's nerves grow calmer. Both Mrs. Crane and Julie tried to soothe him, but he was jumpy and his mouth twitched spasmodically.

The women endeavored to change the subject and talked of other things, whereupon Thorpe sat, brooding,—his dark, handsome face strained and despairful.

"Now, McClellan," Julie said, at last, decidedly, "it's awful enough, goodness knows, but I'll go crazy if you sit there like that any longer! Let's think what's to be done. In the first place, there's Carly to be considered. She's worse hit than you are. Oh, I know you and Gilbert were great friends and all that,—but I think he and Carly were more than friends."

"Julie," said her mother, "don't assume more than you know. Carly hasn't forgotten Peter,—of that I'm sure."

"No; and I don't say there was anything definite between her and Gil Blair, but I think it would have come in time. Gilbert was crazy over her, even before they all went on that trip, and when Peter didn't come back, I think Gilbert felt he had a right to win Carly if he could."

"Oh, he had right enough," Mrs. Crane conceded, "but—I suppose I'm a bit jealous of my son's memory. However, I'm sorry for poor little Carly, if she did care for Gilbert in that way."

And then Carlotta came in. Shelby was with her; he had heard the news and had gone straight to Carlotta's home, and they had come over to the Cranes' together.

Carlotta's eyes were red with weeping, but she was even more indignant than sad.

"Who could have killed Gilbert?" she cried, "and why should any one do so?"

"Killed him!" cried Julie, "what *do* you mean?"

"Why, yes,—haven't you heard? Gilbert was poisoned."

"Oh, Carlotta! Who said so?"

"Kit told me;—tell them about it,—I can't."

So Shelby told them.

"Mr. Crane telephoned me," he said, "only about half an hour ago. He said the doctor found that Gilbert was poisoned, either by himself——"

"Oh, he never did it himself!" Carlotta cried out. "Why should he? He was just on the eve of the great competition,—and he was so excited about it, and so hopeful,—it's absurd to say he killed himself!"

"Of course it is," agreed Julie. "But are they sure it was poison? Mac thought it was acute indigestion,—or a stroke, or something like that."

"No," Shelby said. "Mr. Crane said there was no doubt about it, I mean about the poisoning. But don't be too sure that Gilbert didn't take it himself. It might have been by mistake, you know. And anyway it's a mistake to theorize much until we know more of the details. I'm going up to Blair's place. Coming along, Thorpe?"

"No,—no,—I don't believe I will,—I'll stay here a while, if Mrs. Crane will let me."

"Of course," said Mrs. Crane, in her kind, motherly way, "Mac is all broken up. And no wonder! The shock of finding Gilbert dead——"

"Oh, Mr. Thorpe, did you make the discovery?" exclaimed Carlotta. "How awful! I don't wonder you're upset. Yes, Kit, you go up to Gilbert's. There may be something you can do."

Shelby went away, and when he reached the studio the first one to greet him was Mr. Crane.

"Hello, Shelby, I'm glad you came. This is a bad business."

"Tell me all about it,—I know only the main fact,—of Gilbert's death."

"Yes, that's the main fact, and the next one in importance is that the boy was poisoned. It's not known whether he took the poison himself or whether——"

"But how? I mean, what are the circumstances?"

"Come on in,—the police are here and the doctor. Listen to them."

The two went into the familiar studio, the big room where Blair and his friends had so often forgathered with jests and laughter.

There were two doctors there and two or three men from the Police Department.

The Medical Examiner was talking.

"It's one of those cases," he said, "where there seem to be no clews at all. The autopsy revealed the mere fact that Mr. Blair was poisoned by prussic acid, taken into the stomach. But there is no evidence in the way of a glass or container of any sort, there is no odor of prussic acid about his lips, no real reason to suspect foul play, and yet no apparent reason to think he killed himself. It may have been an accident, yet I can see no real evidence of that. It's mysterious from the very lack of anything suspicious."

"Was he—was he in bed?" asked Shelby, who had heard no detail of Thorpe's finding the body.

"Yes," said Doctor Middleton, the Examiner. "It seems his room-mate found him, in bed, in his night-wear, and immediately called the doorman of the house."

"And then Thorpe lit out," remarked Detective Weston. "I want to see him."

"Oh, Thorpe's all right," said Mr. Crane. "He's down at my house. I'll vouch for him. You needn't look that way for the criminal,—if there is a criminal."

"I should say not!" declared Shelby. "McClellan Thorpe and Mr. Blair were the greatest friends."

"But I can't think Gilbert was killed," Mr. Crane went on. "Seems to me if that were the case, there'd be some evidence of an intruder. And as Gilbert has no friends,—I mean no relatives or family in the city, I'll take up the matter myself. I'd like a thorough investigation, not so much to prove there was a criminal as to prove there wasn't one. I don't think there was, but I'd like a search made for any light that can be thrown on the matter."

"Oh, we'll investigate all right," said Weston; "I think somebody bumped the man off. I don't see any possibility for an accident, but it's more like suicide to me."

"Let's look around a bit," said Shelby. "I'm with you, Mr. Crane, in assuming responsibility. Why, who is there to take charge of Gilbert's things,—his estate?"

"It's hardly a big enough matter to call an estate," Crane said; "of course, I know more or less of Blair's affairs, and he wasn't by any means affluent. Indeed, his hopes of the prize in the coming competition represented his chief asset."

"Thought he'd get a prize, did he?" said Weston, "for what?"

"For his architectural design," Crane answered. "He was working hard, and was hopeful. That's why I feel sure he never killed himself."

"Here are his designs," said Shelby, as he opened a big portfolio. "Why don't you take these, Mr. Crane, and take them home with you. They're really valuable."

"Of course they are,—I'll do that," agreed the older man. "Blair has a sister, somewhere out West. If anything comes of the drawings, it will be hers."

"Can you get in touch with his family?" asked Middleton.

"Don't know anything about them," Crane returned. "I suppose there must be letters or an address book or some such matters in Blair's desk. Thorpe may know more about it than I do."

"Thorpe may know a lot of things," suggested Weston. "Better get him up here, I say."

"All right," Benjamin Crane said, after a moment's pause. "He's down at my house,—I'll telephone him to come up here now."

But when connection was made it transpired that Thorpe had left the Crane house and nobody knew where he was.

"Looks bad," said Weston, shortly. "Why'd he run away?"

"See here, Mr. Weston," Crane said, "if you've any suspicion against McClellan Thorpe just put it out of your mind. He had no hand in Mr. Blair's death——"

"I didn't say he had."

"I know you didn't, but you implied it, and I want to quash any such suggestion at once."

"It's absurd," Shelby agreed. "You don't know the friendship that existed between the two men. Why, they were fellow architects and have lived here together for over two years. They were like brothers."

"That's all right, but why did Thorpe run away?"

"He hasn't run away!" Crane said, "what a ridiculous charge! Merely because he left my house, you say he's run away! He's probably on his way up here. This is his home."

"Well, until he gets here, I'll look around his room a bit," Weston remarked, and as he went into Thorpe's bedroom, Crane followed.

There was nothing sinister there. Merely the usual appointments, and rather plain ones, for the young architects were not of luxurious tastes or means.

With a practiced eye and deft hand, Weston went through dresser drawers, and cupboard shelves. Looked into the books on the night table, and in a short time had satisfied himself that there was no evidence apparent, so far.

Into the bathroom next, they all went. This the two men shared, and the detective scrutinized the glasses and brushes that were on shelves, either side of the wash stand. They were of tidy appearance and presented merely the array that might be expected.

Weston sniffed hard at the glasses, but could detect no untoward odors, nor any sign of poison or drugs of any sort.

The small white cupboard on the wall showed only a few bottles containing toilet appurtenances and simple medicines.

"Witch Hazel, Peroxide, Talcum powder, Cholera mixture and soda mints," he said, from the various labels,—"hello, here's laudanum! How about that?"

"No," Doctor Middleton declared, "it wasn't laudanum poisoning. It was prussic acid. The effects are quite different, and there's no mistaking them. I don't know what the young men were doing with laudanum, but it wasn't that that killed Mr. Blair."

"Curious, to have poison around at all," said Shelby, musingly.

"Gives a hint of intended suicide," suggested Weston. "Though not necessarily——"

"I should say not!" broke in Benjamin Crane. "Gilbert Blair wasn't coward enough to take his own life for any reason. Why, he was my son's friend. It was an accident,—and the fact of finding that other poison about, points toward accident, to my mind."

"Just how do you make that out, Mr. Crane?" asked Weston, with a slight smile.

"Why"—began Crane, a little lamely—"I'm not sure that I can explain, but it appeared to me that if Blair had one poison in his possession, he might have had the other, and——"

"How do you know this laudanum was Mr. Blair's possession?" asked Weston. "Might it not have been Mr. Thorpe's?"

"How you hark back to Thorpe!" exclaimed Crane, with real petulance. "I wish you'd stop it, Weston. If you've a definite suspicion that he killed Gilbert Blair, say so, but don't throw out these silly hints."

"Nothing especially silly about them, Mr. Crane," the detective was quite unruffled, "only I hold that the poison

we've just found is quite as likely to be Mr. Thorpe's as
Mr. Blair's. That's all."

"Of course it is," Shelby said, placatingly, "but that's
neither here nor there. If you have reason to think Mr.
Blair was murdered, you've reason to look for the
criminal. But I don't think you've proved it was not an
accident, and until you do, it's well to be careful how you
throw suspicion about."

"It's not so easy to prove an accident,—or a murder,
either,—when there's practically no clew to be found.
Therefore, it's our duty to question any one who can give
any material evidence, especially one who was
presumably the last one to see Mr. Blair alive."

"Except the murderer,—if there was one," said Shelby.

"Yes, and if he was not the murderer himself,"
grunted Weston.

"Send for that doorman," said Middleton, a bit curtly.
"Let's get somewhere."

Hastings, being summoned, appeared, and told all he
knew, which was little, and all he surmised, which was
more.

"Yes," he said, "Mr. Thorpe called me, this morning,
and when I came, he was all of a shiver. He sat on the
edge of that chair there, and his teeth chattered and his
voice shook——"

"Small wonder!" said Crane. "Mac is a very nervous
man, and a shock such as he must have had——"

"Go on, Hastings," ordered Doctor Middleton.

"Well, Mr. Thorpe said Mr. Blair was ill, and told me
to go in and see him. Now, of course, Mr. Thorpe knew
Mr. Blair was dead, but he said he was ill. Why did he do
that?"

"Tell your story," said Crane, scowling at him. "Don't
ask fool questions as you go along!"

"Yes, sir. Well, I went in and I saw Mr. Blair was
dead. And I told Mr. Thorpe so, and he didn't seem
surprised, but he was all of a blue funk, and he said,
'Well,—get a doctor—or whatever is the thing to do.' Just

like that. He didn't show any grief or any sorrow,—only just seemed scared to death."

"And he didn't show any surprise?" This from Middleton.

"Of course he didn't!" Crane cried; "of course he knew Blair was dead when he called Hastings. I know Thorpe, and he's a most nervous temperament. And when he called for help, as of course he had to do, it was the most natural thing in the world for him to say that Mr. Blair was ill. Nor would he be apt to show his grief then and there. He was stunned, and moreover, he's not the man to talk over his sorrow with the janitor! I say Thorpe acted as any of us would do in the same circumstances. Now, I for one, object to having him misjudged."

"You're a good champion, Mr. Crane," said Doctor Middleton, "and I don't blame you for standing up for your friend. But he'll have to speak for himself,—Mr. Thorpe will,—and the sooner we get hold of him the better."

"I agree to all that," Crane replied, "all I ask is that he shall not be condemned unheard."

"That's reasonable enough," granted Middleton, "but we must get hold of him soon."

"He'll come back here," Mr. Crane assured them. "He hasn't run away, as you seem to think, but he has a natural aversion to this place, and I shouldn't be surprised if he stayed away for a few days."

"A few days! Where would he stay?" asked the Examiner.

"Probably at his Club."

"Which Club? I'll call it up and see if he's there now," Weston said, briskly.

"The Artists' Club. Call it, and they'll tell you something about him, I'm sure."

Weston called the Club and received word that Thorpe was there.

"Ask him to speak to me," he ordered, and in a moment he was talking to Thorpe himself.

"Yes, I'll come home right away," Thorpe agreed, when urgently invited to do so.

"I told you so," said Crane, triumphantly; "that man had no thought of running away, but he dreads this place just now. He's of a sensitive, nervous nature, and I hope, Mr. Weston, you'll be decent to him. No third degree manners,—that won't help with McClellan Thorpe."

They all remained awaiting Thorpe's return. Shelby busied himself looking over some of Blair's books and papers, while Benjamin Crane talked to Dr. Middleton.

He rather liked the Medical Examiner, but he did not at all admire detective Weston or his ways. So he endeavored to give Doctor Middleton a mental picture of Thorpe, and prepare him for an interview that should temper justice with mercy, or at least, consideration.

Weston spent the time prowling round Blair's bedroom in search of clews. But his keen glances could find no single thing that gave any hint of means or reason for suicide, nor any that suggested an accident.

"Wherefore," he concluded to himself, "it's a murder. No clew, means a careful removal of any clew,—and a mighty clever criminal at that. Maybe it wasn't friend Thorpe, but a few words with him will convince me one way or the other."

Thorpe came, and though his expression was inscrutable and his face set and stern, it seemed to those who knew him best that he was trying to hold himself together and not give way to his nervousness.

"Take a seat, Mr. Thorpe," Doctor Middleton said, courteously, after Crane had introduced them; "we expect from you a straightforward account of all you can tell us of your experiences this morning."

"Why should my account be other than straightforward?" Thorpe said, breathing hard, and making an evident effort at self-control. "I have nothing to conceal, and if I seem distraught, it is, I dare say, not astonishing."

"Now, Mac," Mr. Crane said, kindly, "don't bristle. We're all your friends, and we only want you——"

"Good heavens, Mr. Crane, why do you take that conciliatory attitude? I've no confession to make,— I— I didn't kill Blair——"

"Why do you say that?" cried Weston. "Who even hinted that you killed Mr. Blair? Why do you think anybody killed him?"

"Why do you?" countered Thorpe, turning an angry glance at the detective.

"I haven't said I did."

"Not in so many words,—but you imply it. I tell you I didn't kill him! I *didn't!*"

Thorpe was not excited of manner, he was very calm, but his blazing eyes and quivering mouth, and his intensity, rather than force of speech gave him the effect of intense excitement.

"Don't deny or assert, Mr. Thorpe," said Middleton, coldly. "Just tell your story. At what time did you rise?"

"About ten o'clock," was the short reply.

"And then?"

"Then I bathed, shaved and dressed just as usual. I generally dress before Mr. Blair, and I thought nothing of his silence."

"His bedroom door was closed?"

"Yes; then, after I was dressed and about to go out to my breakfast, I called to him through the door."

"What did you say?"

"I can't repeat the exact words, but it was only to the effect of 'good-by, old chap,' or maybe, 'I'm off, Blair,' or something of the sort."

"And you went on?"

"I didn't hear him reply,—he usually says, 'All right, Mac,' so I repeated my call. Then, when he didn't respond that time, I knocked at his door."

"Fearing something was wrong?"

"N-no,—not wrong,— I think I just wanted him to say something——"

"Why were you so anxious he should say something?" This last from Weston, with a direct glance.

"Why, good Lord, man," Thorpe's eyes blazed, "because I am accustomed to a reply, and when it didn't come, I naturally wondered why."

"Didn't you think he might merely be asleep?"

"I didn't think anything about that. I acted on impulse. I didn't hear him, and I wanted to see him."

"And you did? You opened the door?"

"Yes, after I knocked twice,—then I— I opened his door."

"It was not locked?"

"No; we never lock our bedroom doors."

"Go on,—and then?"

"Then"—Thorpe spoke slowly, as if choosing his words—"then, I saw him lying in the bed,—still,—as if asleep. I went closer, and I saw by the look on his face that he was dead."

"You knew that at once?" asked Middleton. "You didn't think he was only asleep——"

"No,—the pallor was unmistakable——"

"Have you often looked upon death?"

"Never before,—except at a funeral."

"And yet you knew at once it was death you saw,—not sleep. That is remarkable, Mr. Thorpe."

Thorpe met Middleton's eyes, and then his own fell.

"I can't help that, Doctor," he said; "I was sure,—that is,—almost sure Mr. Blair was dead."

"Yet you called Hastings and told him Mr. Blair was ill."

"Yes,—I couldn't seem to say the—the other——"

"Why did you kill him, Mr. Thorpe?"

"I— I kill him! Oh, I didn't!— I told you I didn't!"

"Yes; but we can't believe you."

CHAPTER 10: EVIDENCE

The few days following Gilbert Blair's death were like a nightmare to his friends. A search of his papers had revealed a probable address of his mother, but a telegram sent there had as yet brought no reply and though a letter was despatched, no answer could be expected to that for a week or more.

Meantime, by general consent, Benjamin Crane took charge of Blair's affairs. The funeral took place in an undertaker's establishment and the body was placed in a receiving vault, until Blair's people could be heard from. His immediate possessions remained in the studio rooms, for the lease had still six months to run, and the police objected to any removal of the dead man's effects. It was practically impossible to seal them up as Thorpe occupied the same rooms, but a strict surveillance was kept, and Weston doggedly asserted he would yet track down the murderer.

For no one could doubt Blair had been murdered. On the eve of the prize competition, in which he was so deeply interested,—on the eve, as he hoped, of being engaged to Carlotta Harper, whom he loved, full of life and energy, why should he kill himself? It was impossible to accept the theory of suicide, and the detectives were hard at work on the case.

McClellan Thorpe was suspected, but as there was no evidence against him, save his indubitable and exclusive opportunity, he had not as yet been arrested.

"His opportunity was not exclusive," Mr. Crane contended. "Those studio apartments are not burglar proof! Anybody might have got in during the night and administered the poison."

"No," Weston objected. "It would be practically impossible for any one to go into those rooms, force or persuade Blair to swallow poison and get away without being heard by Mr. Thorpe or without leaving any trace of his presence."

"Well, look here, Weston," Mr. Crane spoke very seriously, "you know me well enough to know I've no notion of evading justice for anybody. But knowing McClellan Thorpe as I do, and knowing his peculiar temperament, I wish you'd let him alone,—at least, until you have a bit of indisputable evidence."

"I've got it, Mr. Crane."

"What?"

The two were sitting in Benjamin Crane's library, where they often met to talk over the case. Julie was present, for she wanted to know every detail of any discovery that might be made.

"I don't believe it!" she flared out at the detective's statement.

"Yes, Miss Crane," Weston said, "I found a pretty suspicious circumstance to-day. Nothing less than a very small bottle, without cork or label, but smelling unmistakably of prussic acid."

"Where was it?" demanded Crane.

"Hidden in an old and unused paint-box of McClellan Thorpe's."

"Where was the paint-box?"

"'Way back, on a cupboard shelf. Pushed back, behind a pile of old books."

"Planted evidence," suggested Crane. "The real criminal put it there to incriminate Mr. Thorpe."

"Not a chance!" said Weston, smiling. "I've had that place watched too closely for that, sir! Nobody could get in to plant evidence, or to do anything else without being seen by my men. No, sir, that bottle in Mr. Thorpe's paint-box was put there by his own hand, and it will prove his undoing."

"But it's absurd!" flashed Julie. "Mr. Thorpe never killed his friend,—but if he had done so, he wouldn't be fool enough to leave such evidence around!"

"He couldn't help himself, Miss Crane. When he used the bottle that night, he had to secrete it somewhere, and since then he has been too closely watched to dare to take it from its hiding-place and dispose of it."

"But I don't see how he could have done it," Crane objected. "How could he persuade Blair to take a dose of poison?"

"Oh, in lots of ways. Say, they had a highball or that,—all he had to do was to drop the tiniest speck from the little vial into the drink. He could easily do that unobserved. Anyway, he did do it. Then, of course, afterward, he had ample chance to clean the glasses and remove every trace of crime, except that he had to conceal the bottle. This he did in the most obvious way. Exactly the way any one would try to secrete such a thing. The bottle had been emptied and washed, but that poison has such an enduring odor that it is practically impossible to eliminate it entirely. But there's the fact, Mr. Crane, now, unless another suspect can be found, it's all up with Mr. Thorpe."

"Then we'll find another suspect!" exclaimed Julie.

"Go ahead, Miss. I'll investigate your new man, as soon as you name him. That's the important part of this affair, there's no chance of another suspect. No one has been so much as thought of——"

"That doorman?" said Julie.

"Nixy! He had no motive, no opportunity,—and there's not the slightest reason to suspect him."

"Some outsider, then," went on Julie, desperately, "some fellow artist, who feared Gilbert would win that prize——"

"Miss Crane, you must know that's the motive attributed to Mr. Thorpe. You must know that he and Mr. Blair were rivals in that competition and——"

Julie's eyes flashed fire. "And you mean to say that he killed his friend,—his chum,—in order to be sure of winning the prize!"

"That's the motive we're assuming. But there was doubtless a scrap,—a row about the pictures or drawings,—in fact,— I hate to tell you these things, but we have learned that there was bad blood between the two men, for each thought the other had imitated his own ideas. This brought about more or less dissension, and— well, probably both men lost their temper, and real hatred ensued."

Weston tried to adapt his language so as to spare Julie's feelings as much as possible, for the girl was highly wrought up, and he was genuinely sorry for her. He knew of the state of things between her and Thorpe, knew, too, that it explained Benjamin Crane's determination to free Thorpe from suspicion, if it could be done.

But Crane was staggered by the disclosure of the hidden vial.

"It's a clew," he said, but he spoke slowly and thoughtfully.

"Yes, it's a clew," agreed Weston, "and it will convict the criminal. The label,—if it ever had one,—has been washed off. The cork is missing,—and, by the way, if that cork could be found it would help a lot! But all the same, I've a notion I can trace that bottle to its source."

"How?" asked Crane. "Is it of a peculiar shape or style?"

"No; just a common, ordinary two-ounce bottle, such as most druggists use all the time. But there's no name blown in it,—that's important, for many dealers have their names on their glassware, and a blank bottle is conspicuous of itself."

"Conspicuous by its rarity,—but not therefore traceable," said Mr. Crane.

"Perhaps so,—by elimination——"

"Nonsense!" Julie cried; "you can't trace it, and you know it! You're just making believe,—you're what do you call it? framing a case! you're railroading McClellan Thorpe to prison! I won't have it! Father, surely you can do something! You *must!*"

Stifling her sobs, Julie ran out of the room.

There was an uncomfortable silence and then Benjamin Crane said:

"You see what a hard position I'm in, Weston."

"Yes, sir."

"But of course," Crane sighed deeply, "justice must be done,—only I beg of you, Weston, use every effort to find another suspect,—a logical one,—now, don't misunderstand me! I mean, if there can possibly be a doubt of Thorpe's guilt, and a chance of another man's guilt,—for Heaven's sake find that other man!"

"Not a chance."

"But, at least, keep an open mind. And spare no expense. Get a special detective,—a big one,—there now, don't bristle! I don't suppose you think yourself the cleverest in the world, do you? Don't you admit any superior? If so, get him; if not, then prove your own worth. I repeat, I want no undue favor shown to McClellan Thorpe, but if he is not the guilty man, then I want you to move heaven and earth to find the real criminal. Can't you conceive, Weston, of a murderer so clever as to have committed the crime, planted the vial as evidence against Thorpe and made his escape leaving no clew?"

"I can conceive of such a thing, sir, as I can conceive of a ghost,—but there is no evidence for either conception."

"Evidence enough for ghosts, Weston! Haven't you read my book?"

"Oh, I clean forgot that book you wrote, Mr. Crane. No, I haven't read it, but my folks have, and I dare say you do believe in spooks. But, come, now, you don't believe a spook killed Mr. Blair, do you, sir?"

"No,—and yet, it is within the bounds of possibility—"

"Not as the police count possibility! There's small chance of any human agency other than Mr. Thorpe, but far less chance of a supernatural agent! I'll be getting along, Mr. Crane, if you're going off on that track."

"Hold on, Weston, I'm in earnest about this special detective. Suppose I engage a private one. Can you and he work in harmony?"

"Oh, yes, I'm not pig-headed. So long as he don't interfere too much, or get me into any scrapes with his highfalutin tricks,—which they all have, go ahead and get him. I'll do my own duty, as I see it and as it's dictated to me by Headquarters; but if you want to engage a dozen private detectives, there's no law against it. And, sir, I'm free to confess I feel mighty sorry for that pretty daughter of yours, and if anybody else can save her man for her, when I can't—why, let him at it!"

"Good for you, Weston, I hoped you'd be above petty jealousy. Go on, now, and see if you can't connect up that empty vial with somebody whose name isn't Thorpe,— and, I say, you're not going to arrest him yet, are you?"

"Not just yet,—but,—well, I'll let you know—soon, where we stand."

His visitor gone, Benjamin Crane put on his hat and went at once to see Madame Parlato. He had acquired the habit of an interview with her when anything bothered him, and his faith in her powers was unshaken.

His request for a *seance* was granted, for since the book of Benjamin Crane's had made such a success, the medium was besieged with patrons, yet she always gave Crane the preference over other sitters.

Admitted to the private sanctum, Crane told the Madame he wished to learn anything possible concerning the death of Gilbert Blair.

The medium went into a trance as usual, and after a short interval, announced in her low monotone that the spirit of Peter Crane was present.

"My boy," said Crane, eagerly, "do you know who killed Blair?"

"Yes, father," came the reply, through the voice of Madame Parlato; "do not seek further than you already know."

"You mean it was——"

Benjamin Crane hesitated. He was a cautious man, and often as he had had this sort of interviews with Peter's spirit, he was always particular to give no information unnecessarily.

"Yes,—dad,—it was."

"Well, who? who, Peter?"

"Must I say the name?"

"Yes, boy. But only if you're sure you know. It would be a grave error otherwise."

The medium stirred uneasily, and was silent for a time. Then, with a long drawn sigh, she resumed, "Well, father, if I must tell you, it was Thorpe."

"Oh, Peter, not really!"

"Yes, dad. Don't look any further,—it was Thorpe."

The medium was silent after that. She came out of her trance state, looking a little bewildered.

"Did you get anything?" she asked, for, as she had frequently told her sitter, she herself knew nothing of what transpired while she was unconscious.

"Yes," Crane returned, and knowing there would be no further communication that day, he went home.

He found Thorpe there, discussing the matter with Mrs. Crane and Julie.

"I don't know what to do," Thorpe said, as Mr. Crane joined the group. "I didn't kill Blair,—at least, I don't think I did."

"What does that mean?" Crane asked.

"Only that if I did do it, it was unconsciously."

"In your sleep?"

"No; but under hypnotism. I've not much belief in that sort of thing,—but,—well, you know about occult matters, might it not be possible?"

Benjamin Crane was disappointed. He had hoped for a vigorous denial on Thorpe's part, but this halfway confession seemed to him a mere quibble. He found himself believing the man guilty and that he was using this hypnotism suggestion as a last resort to prove innocence.

"Stop it, father!" Julie cried. "You are thinking Mac did do it, having been hypnotized by somebody! Well, he didn't! and I *know* he didn't and I'll *prove* it!"

"Good talk, Julie, but does it mean anything!" asked her father, giving her a look of gentle sadness.

"I'll make it mean something! That thick-witted detective doesn't know a thing! Now, I don't believe in the hypnotism theory——"

"Why, Julie," said her mother, "I've heard you say you believed in hypnotism!"

"Oh, yes, I do, but I mean not in this case. Nobody hypnotized McClellan to kill Gilbert. I'm sure of that, and I wish you wouldn't repeat it, Mac. People will only laugh at you."

"Well, what are you going to do, my child?" asked her father.

"Oh, I don't know! I'm desperate,— I will find out something!"

"Of course you will, Julie, for I'll help you."

It was Thorpe who spoke, and he seemed to have suddenly acquired a new energy.

"I'm going to turn detective myself," he went on. "We'll work together, Julie, and,— Mr. Crane, if we succeed,— I mean succeed in freeing myself from suspicion——"

"And finding the real criminal," put in Crane with a very serious face.

"Yes, and find the real criminal," but Thorpe's face was less bright, "then, sir, will you give us your blessing?"

"Yes, McClellan," but Crane's voice had no hearty ring, "yes, when you are a free man in every sense of the word, you may take my little girl for your own."

Thorpe gave him a searching look. "I can't help seeing, Mr. Crane," he said, "that you think,—or perhaps I may say, you fear I am guilty. I hope I can prove to you that I am not."

Crane noticed the wording of his speech. Thorpe hoped to prove to him,—but he didn't say he was innocent.

And Benjamin Crane believed the man guilty. Greatly influenced by what he had heard at the *seance* with the medium, Crane was still willing to be convinced to the contrary, but Thorpe's own attitude and words did not carry conviction.

"Well, my children," Crane said at last, "here's my proposition. I can't think your determination to do detective work will produce much fruit. Now, if you like, I'll engage the best detective I can find and put him on the job. What say, Thorpe?"

It was a test question, and Crane eagerly awaited the answer. If Thorpe were really innocent, he would welcome the clever sleuthing that would be likely to unearth the truth.

But he was disappointed to hear Thorpe say, "Not yet, Mr. Crane. Give us a chance. Let me try,—let us try,"— with a glance at Julie—"give us a few days, at least,— then, if we gain nothing,—then bring on your detective."

"But,— I hate to say it, Mac, though I dare say you know it,—you may be arrested any day now."

Thorpe gave a start, and the sudden pallor that came to his face showed how the idea affected him.

"Oh, not that,—hardly that——"

"Yes, it's imminent." Crane thought best to tell him this. "They—they say they've got the goods on you, Mac."

"What—what do you mean by that?"

"Well," Crane couldn't bring himself to tell of the poison bottle, "well, my boy, they say that you and Blair quarreled."

"We did."

"Over the sketches for the prizes?"

"Yes, over those, and over other matters."

"When was this?"

"We'd been scrapping off and on for some time. Nothing very serious. But,—well, when Gilbert implied that I had used his ideas, I—I got mad."

"And saw red?"

"Yes, I suppose that's what they call it."

"The night he—he died?"

"Yes."

"Mac," Benjamin Crane looked grave, "suppose you tell me just what happened that night."

"Well,—we'd all been to the Club to dinner, you know."

"Yes."

"And when we went home, Bob Knight went with us. He was irritating, somehow,—said he heard Blair and I had combined on our work——"

"Why was that annoying?"

"Oh, it implied that Gilbert and I took each other's ideas, or something,— I don't know,—anyway, he stirred us up, and when he went off, Gil and I were touchy. We had some words, and Blair tore up his sketches, a-and— tore up some of mine, too."

"He did! No wonder you were annoyed."

"Yes; they were the ones I had ready,—or, almost ready, to send in."

"Go on," said Crane, briefly.

"Well, there's little more to tell. I went into my bedroom and slammed the door. Yes, I slammed it, for I had lost my temper, and I was mad at Blair."

"And then?"

"I don't know anything more to tell. I heard Blair around the studio for a time, and once I heard his footsteps near my door, as if he wanted to speak to me,— maybe make up,—but he didn't say anything or knock, or call out,—and then, after a time I heard him go into his own bedroom and close the door."

"And you heard nothing through the night?"

"Nothing unusual. The ordinary sounds in the building, of course."

"And you stayed in your room,—in your bed,—till morning?"

"Yes, I did. I sleep very soundly, and I sleep late. The details of the morning, and my finding of Blair,—you know. Don't ask me to recount all that again."

"No; I shan't. Are you going on with your work for the competition?"

"Of course!" Thorpe's face showed surprise at the question. "Why should I not? I rescued the torn sketches from the waste-basket, and I can copy them. I've a good chance at it, I think."

"Now that Blair's out of the running?"

Thorpe looked up angrily, but as suddenly he became calm. "No, Mr. Crane," he said, "not because of that. But because Gilbert can't steal my plans."

"Unpleasant talk, Mac. I don't like that."

"But it's true. Blair did take my ideas——"

"Consciously?"

"I think so. Why, he incorporated in his design, a particular bit of drawing that I had invented and shown to him only a day or two before."

"You must see, McClellan, that your saying that puts a bad face on the whole affair?"

"I suppose it does," and the man again relapsed into moody silence. "Oh, well,—it's all in a lifetime."

"A lifetime that has just ended,—or one still being lived?" Benjamin Crane spoke like an avenging justice, and there was no mistaking his meaning.

But beyond a startled glance, Thorpe made no reply.

CHAPTER 11: CARLOTTA AND THE BOARD

Much as Benjamin Crane desired to believe in Thorpe's innocence it was difficult for him to do so, after the disclosure of the medium, Madame Parlato. In her powers he had absolute faith, of her honesty and sincerity he was entirely confident, and it was largely the accounts of her *seances* that made the bulk of his book about his son's communications with him. The *seances* were frequent, still, and at each one he gained more material for use in a second book.

The book, the one already published, was in its fourth edition and was still having large sales. It was called "A Prophecy Fulfilled," and dealt with the old prophecy of the gypsy,—that Peter should be lost while on a distant journey, should die a terrible death there, but should mysteriously return to his family.

This, Benjamin Crane held, had been accomplished in full. The long journey, the terrible death, were matters of fact, and Mr. and Mrs. Crane believed that the return of their son was equally a matter of fact.

Wherefore, the book was written in a simple, straightforward style, without excitement or exaggeration, and it gave detailed recitals of the happenings at the *seances*.

Needless to say that the medium was besieged with would-be clients, but she accepted very few, for the Cranes claimed most of her time. Not that they were continually in her presence, but the exhaustive nature of her trances made it impossible for her to devote many hours a day to their practice. And Benjamin Crane made it quite worth her while, financially, to reserve for him her peculiar talents.

The sessions brought forth little that was new or different, but the parents never tired of what they implicitly believed was absolute direct communication with their son's spirit through the personality of Madame Parlato.

Criticism, disapproval, even ridicule from their friends and acquaintances moved them not a jot from their faith and trust.

Wiser and better people than we, believe in it,—they would argue,—and it is now so much a part of our lives, that I think we could scarcely live without it.

And so, they went along, cheered and made happy by the communications and fully reconciled thereby to the death of their cherished son.

Julie, though never quite satisfied of the truth of the whole matter, had become more or less imbued with the atmosphere that she lived in, and aside from her own feelings, was glad that her parents could be happy in their grief, even though it were a delusion.

And the popularity of this book brought him absorbing work and many outside interests to Benjamin Crane. Continually, people came to see him, to discuss the question of Continuity, or Life after Death, and to argue for or against the reappearance of departed spirits.

Many of these he saw and learned to like and his circle of acquaintances was continually enlarging.

Naturally, when he discussed matters with them, the subject of Gilbert Blair's death was talked of. Crane was a careful man, and rarely told what happened at his *seances*, save in a general way. For he had learned of the dangers of having his statements misquoted and exaggerated, and as a rule, he was canny enough to let his visitors talk, while he said little.

And from the consensus of opinion thus gathered, he discovered that public sentiment was largely against McClellan Thorpe. This troubled him, for if Thorpe were guilty it was surely Crane's duty to guard his daughter from a criminal. On the other hand, Julie was so deeply in love with Thorpe, and so positive that he was in no way a wrong-doer, that the father's heart was torn.

But his most vital reason for believing in Thorpe's guilt was the message from his son to that effect.

"It rests between our two children," he said to his wife. "Peter tells us Mac is the guilty man,—and Julie tells us he isn't. Now, we must learn the truth. I'm going to get a detective, myself,— I've had a fine one recommended,—and I don't think we need say anything to Julie or Mac about it. They asked for a few days to do some 'detecting' on their own account,—but it won't amount to anything, I feel sure. So I'm going to engage Pennington Wise,—if I can get him. I'm told he's a most successful man, though not one of the 'wizards' or know-it-all variety."

"Very well," Mrs. Crane, as always, agreed; "but don't tell anybody. Need you?"

"Yes, I'll tell Weston. It wouldn't be fair not to. You see, I'm in a peculiar position. I've taken the responsibility of investigating Blair's death, without any real authority, save that of a friend."

"Of course your reason is that Julie cares for him."

"Of course. And I do hope he can be cleared, but if not, it would better be proved against him, and let Julie know it, and get over it."

"Yes," Mrs. Crane sighed. "Poor child, it would go hard with her."

"But she must bear it, if it's the truth. I've hopes of Wise's discovering another criminal."

"Then what about Peter's message?"

"I don't know,—but it's possible Peter may himself be misinformed. You know we've discovered that the disembodied spirits are not omniscient."

In the meantime Carlotta Harper was endeavoring to use her occult powers to solve the mystery of Blair's death.

Carlotta herself was a mystery. Disavowing any especial clairvoyant ability, she yet achieved marvelous results from the Ouija Board.

She scoffed at it herself, yet whenever her finger-tips were on the board it spelled words rapidly and gave messages that were acclaimed as truth by the audience.

One afternoon Shelby was with her, and he, a little timidly, suggested a trial of the Board.

"Why, Kit, I thought you detested it," said Carly, surprised.

"I do; but you're a witch at it, and—suppose it should tell us something about Blair,—something we don't know——"

"You think Mac did it, don't you?" Carly spoke hesitantly, for the two had discussed the subject very little.

"I don't say so, Carly, yet where else is there to look? If you had seen, as I did, how much at odds the two chaps were that evening I dropped in——"

"The night of the dinner?"

"Yes, in the late afternoon. They were rowing no end! Then I went off, but I called for them on the way to the feast,—we always go together,—and Blair was in a regular stew. Nervous,—couldn't get his tie right,—and all that. And—Carly,—what do you think? He asked me if I'd drop you! Think of that! As if I were a sort of man to interfere with a friend's interests! Why, if he'd told me there was anything between you two, of course I should have stepped down and out at once. Was there, Carly?"

"Nothing definite,—no." The girl spoke wearily, pushing back her thick mass of dark, wavy hair. "No, Kit, nothing promised. If he had lived—oh, I don't know. You see, I loved Peter. And I sometimes think I never can care at all for any one else."

"But, dear, Peter's dead and Blair's dead,—and you can't live all your life alone: Just give me a ray of hope, Carly. I won't bother you about it,—only tell me that some time,—maybe——"

"Let it stay at that, Kit. Some time it may be—and now come on,—if you like we'll try the Ouija."

The session was interesting. Carly never, in any circumstances, pushed or guided the board in the very least,—nor did she ever sit with any one whom she suspected of doing so. But with her friends in whom she had perfect confidence, or with acquaintances who, she knew were eagerly wanting to learn, not anxious to tell, she often tried the uncanny thing.

Lightly they rested their finger-tips on the little wooden heart, and after a short wait it began to move.

At Carly's questions, replies came that there was a spirit present and that it was Peter Boots.

Neither of the inquirers was surprised at this, for they had fully expected it. Moreover, both had watched most closely the other's muscles and fingers and wrists, and each was positive the messages, whatever their source, were not the result of human deceit.

After some preliminary talk, Carly said, "You put the questions, Kit."

So Shelby said, "Peter, you know Blair's gone?"

"Yes," returned the board.

"Have you seen him—or I mean, is he with you—in spirit?"

"Yes" came the answer.

"Will he talk to us?"

"No."

"Well—then can you give us a message from him?"

"Yes."

Yes and No are designated on the Ouija Board as words. The movement of the Board toward these was quick, almost jerky.

But when the message was asked for,—when Shelby said, "Will he tell us how he died?" there was a pause and the Board moved aimlessly about.

At last, Carly said, "Peter, was Gilbert killed?"

"Yes," came the quick reply.

"Do you know who killed him?"

"Yes."

"Who was it?"

Carly shot out the question quickly, and immediately the board moved to T. From that, as the two breathlessly waited, the pointer very slowly spelled Thorpe.

The word did not go smoothly,—the board swung round in large loops, but paused positively at each letter, and then started slowly to the next.

"You didn't push, Kit?" Carly asked, but more from force of habit than any doubt of him.

"Of course not. Nobody could push with you watching, nor was there any reason why I should. Did you?"

"Of course not. Don't let's ask each other that. We're both honest. But you know, Kit, Mr. Crane had a communication from Peter and he said Thorpe did it. But Mr. Crane thinks maybe Peter doesn't know."

"Let's try to get Blair's spirit."

They tried,—if receptive waiting can be called trying,—and at last they succeeded in receiving the information that Gilbert Blair's spirit was present.

"Will you tell us who killed you?" Carly asked at once, fearing lest he go away.

Slowly the pointer moved away from the letter T. But after a series of swirls it stopped definitely at M.

"Go on," said Carly, in a whisper.

A long swing of aimless motions and then a stop at A.

The next stop was at C, and then the board would move no more.

Carly sighed, and took her hands off.

"Well, there's the message, Kit. You know Gilbert always called him Mac,—now what do you think of Ouija?"

"I don't know what to think, Carly. Mayn't it be only that Thorpe was in both our minds, and that we subconsciously——"

"Oh, well, if you're going to take that tack, there's no more to be said. It's easy enough to say that,—but how can the dead send messages if the human beings always say,—oh, subconscious pushing!"

"But, are you so anxious to believe in Thorpe's guilt?"

"Not that,—but I want to know. Julie's devoted to him, and if he's a—a murderer, Julie must be saved from him. If he isn't,—we must find it out, and give him to Julie free and clear of suspicion."

"We! Are you responsible for Julie's affairs?"

"Yes, in so far as I can help. You say, everybody says, that I have occult powers. If so, I must use them to help,—if they really do help. But how can I be sure?"

"I don't know. But I think, perhaps, you'd better leave the whole occult business alone. It's uncanny if it's real, and it's foolishness if it's faked."

"I think Mr. Crane is going to get a special detective," Carly said, "but, oh, my gracious, I forgot I promised not to tell that. So don't tell anybody else. I don't suppose they'd mind you knowing."

"Who's the man?"

"I think his name is Wise,—good name for a detective!"

"Never heard of him. But, let's hope he clears Mac."

"Yes, and finds the real murderer. Do you know I can't realize Gilbert's gone,—even yet."

"Don't think about him, Carly. It can't do any good, and it only makes you sad and morbid. Let me tell you of my hopes and fears, mayn't I?"

"Of course, go ahead."

"Well, I'm getting up a big,—a really big enterprise."

"What?"

"I hope you won't disapprove, but it's in the Moving Picture business."

"Why should I disapprove?"

"Oh, some people sniff at M. P's. But this is a really big, fine production."

"Are you the producer?"

"Yes; don't tell it outside, yet. You see, I've written a big story,—a picturesque thriller,—and critics who've read it, think it's a wonder. Now, it's too big to give to anybody,— I mean, it would be foolish for me merely to get a royalty,—so I'm going to put it on, myself."

"Good, Kit, I'm glad to hear it. I always thought you had it in you to be some sort of an organizer or producer, in some important way."

"Yes, I've always had that ambition. Well, this is a great yarn! I want to read it to you some time. Marvelous pictures,—they're being made now. And that's not all of it,— I mean to make it into a book——"

"You can't write a book!"

"If I can't I'll get it written,—but the plot is such a wonder,—and the scenes!"

"Up in Labrador, I'll bet!"

"Yes, they are, Carly. And corkers! Well, I figure to have the book and the pictures sprung on an unsuspecting public simultaneously,—and afterward,— maybe, it will be made into a real play!"

"And after that, into a Light Opera,—and after that, into Grand Opera?"

Carly's tone was mocking, but her smile was sweet and approving, and Kit beamed at her.

"I knew you'd be interested! I want you to hear the plot soon,—and would you like to go to the studios?"

"Where they're making the Labrador pictures?"

"Yes; they're faked, of course. No sense in going up there to take them. I know the stuff so well, I can get it up right here."

"Oh, Kit, you ought to have the real scenes."

"No; it isn't necessary. Snow's easy enough to manage. But the plot's the thing! Carly, it's a peach! And then, it's all done up with real artistry. No crude, raw scenes. All softened with lights and shades and colors; and everything,—even realism, sacrificed to beauty. It will be the success of the season, the talk of the town, and it will make my reputation forever."

"When will it be put on?"

"Soon, now, I hope. Well, I mean in a month or so. I'd like to say the middle of May, and think perhaps I can. It will run all summer and doubtless longer."

"And you don't want me to tell of this?"

"Not quite yet, Carly. I'll let you know when you may."

*   *   *   *   *

And so, when, after Shelby had gone, and Julie and Thorpe came, Carly said nothing of the plans for the great Moving Picture.

Nor did she tell of the Ouija Board experiences she and Shelby had had. In fact, Carly said little, preferring to let her guests talk.

And they did.

"We're detecting," Julie began, and Thorpe, his eyes harassed and gloomy, had to smile at Julie's enthusiasm.

"Can I help?" Carly asked, with a loving glance at her friend.

"I hope so,—but not with your old Ouija Board. I hate it!"

"Wait till I suggest it," Carly smiled, for she saw Julie was in no mood for argument. "What can I do?"

"Only advise. I don't think you're a medium, Carly, but I do think you have sort of queer powers. Now a queer thing has happened to me. This morning, on my bureau, there lay a note,—here it is." She handed a folded paper to Carlotta.

It read: "Dear little sister. You *must* give up old Mac. He did for Gilbert. Peter Boots."

Carly stared at the note.

"It's in Peter's own writing!" she said; "what can it mean?"

"It means fraud!" Julie exclaimed. "I know that's no note from Peter! It is in his writing——"

"But so exactly his writing!" Carly said, "nobody could have written that but Peter himself. Oh, Julie!"

"Now, stop, Carly! Don't you say it's really a materialization of a note from Peter! It can't be! I'm afraid to show it to mother or Dad, for I know they'll say it's really from him,—and I won't believe it."

"You won't believe it's from Peter, because you don't want to believe what it says,—isn't that it?"

Carly looked at Thorpe, though she spoke to Julie.

"Partly," Julie admitted; "but anyway, I can't believe that Peter,—my dead brother,—put that real, paper note on my dresser!"

"If it had said Mac didn't kill Gilbert, would you believe it then?" Carly asked.

Julie stared at her, as she took in the question.

"Yes," she said at last, "in that case, I'd want to believe,—but I don't see how I could——"

"Oh, you could, all right," Carly said, "if it meant Mac's innocence was thereby established."

"I'm out for justice," Thorpe said; "I hate to hurt Julie's feelings, but that note doesn't interest me at all,— one way or the other. You see, if it's a fake,—and I can't help thinking it is, it's somewhat in my favor, for if faked must it not have been done by the real murderer, trying to put the blame on me? And if it's real—but, I never discuss that sort of thing at all. I'm not a believer,—as the Cranes believe, and yet, feeling toward the Crane family as I do, I refuse to combat their beliefs or principles. So, as I say, I leave the note out of my consideration. And, yet, Carlotta, I do want your opinion as to the genuineness of the handwriting, because you know Peter's fist so well,—and you're even less likely to be deceived than his family."

Carly scrutinized the note again.

"It seems to me it must be Peter's writing," she said at last. "Those long tails to the final letters of the words, those are characteristic. And it's—yes, it's unmistakably his."

"All right," Thorpe sighed. "I just wanted to know, for Mr. Crane will know of it sooner or later, and I'm sure he'll identify it as Peter's writing.

"And it surely is," Julie added, again staring at the paper.

"But, Julie, it's *too* absurd!" Second thoughts convinced Carly of this. "How could such a thing happen?"

"I don't know how it could, but it did," Julie said, doggedly. "And so, Carly, I feel, as Mac says, there's no attention to be paid to this note. If—mind I say *if*—Peter sent it, why then Peter thinks Mac did something that he didn't do, that's all. I know Mac is innocent, and so I shall say nothing of this note to any one, and you mustn't either."

"I won't," Carly smiled to herself as she realized how many secrets she was accumulating, "but you will, Julie. You can't keep that from your father, even though you mean to."

"Yes, I can, if to tell of it would cast a straw of evidence against Mac! You see, Carly, we've got to find the real criminal, and I'd rather do it myself than get a new detective on the job."

Carly knew this was because Julie feared the astuteness of the new detective. Which, in turn, meant that Julie, herself, feared Mac's guilt. Oh, it was a tightly closing net round Mac, as she saw it!

"I wish I could help," she found herself saying, most unconsciously, so deeply was she thinking. "But, Julie, you two can do nothing. What are you expecting to accomplish?"

"Success," Thorpe made reply. "Complete success. It may sound absurd, but I think that note is a help to my cause rather than hindrance!"

"I think so, too," said Carlotta.

CHAPTER 12: WISE AND ZIZI

"Well, Julie, my little girl, the jig is up."

Thorpe spoke despairingly, and Julie knew only too well what he meant.

"They're—they're going——"

"Yes, they're going to arrest me. This is the last call I can pay you."

Julie didn't break down and cry, nor indeed did she show great emotion of any sort. She set her curved red lips firmly and said, with an air of determination:

"I'm not sure, Mac, that it isn't better so. I mean now we've something definite to work against. Father's going to get that Mr. Wise, and he'll soon get you out of—out of—oh, Mac, will they put you in prison? In a cell?"

"Yes, dear, until the trial. You see, that little bottle did it for me."

"And somebody put that in your old paint-box! Who did it, Mac?"

"Hastings is the only one I can think of. That man never liked me— I don't know why, but he never did. And he adored Gilbert——"

"You don't think he killed Gilbert, then?"

"Oh, Lord, no! He was always fond of him. But he wants to get me in bad, and so I think he planted that bottle. It must have been planted, Julie, I never put it there. I never had it in my possession."

"Who did kill Gilbert?"

"I've no idea, but I don't think it was anybody we know. I'm inclined to the belief that it was some enemy, of long standing. You know Gilbert Blair's past life was by no means an open book to his friends. He had turned-down pages that we never knew about or inquired into. It would not have been impossible for some one to get into his room in the night——"

"And give him poison? Not likely!"

"But it must have been something of the sort, Julie. Blair never killed himself."

"No, I suppose not. Oh, Mac, how unfortunate that you and he quarreled so much. Otherwise they wouldn't have suspected you at all."

"Yes, they would. It's opportunity they consider, exclusive opportunity."

"And that empty bottle! I should think they'd see that's a plant!"

"They don't see anything an inch away from their noses! I'm the nearest suspect to hang a charge on, so they choose me."

Thorpe wasn't pettish, but he was discouraged and unstrung. He knew that his arrest, which was imminent, was, in part, due to the assertions of the medium and the Ouija Board. These secrets had leaked out somehow, and though the detective, Weston, would have scorned to acknowledge it, he had been more or less biased in his estimates of other evidence by what he had heard of supernatural communications.

But of this Thorpe hesitated to speak to Julie. For it was her father who had brought those things about, and while Thorpe had no use for the whole mediumistic business, he rarely said so to the Crane family.

And the note that purported to be from Peter, he believed a bare-faced fraud. He couldn't understand it, nor imagine how it had been managed, but he would not believe that it was the work of the dead Peter Crane.

And so, he submitted helplessly to arrest, for there was no way to prove his innocence. He had tried "detective work" on his own account, but it amounted to nothing. The police held that it was an "open and shut" case, and that Thorpe must have been the murderer.

Benjamin Crane, though all unwilling to condemn Thorpe, was, of course, greatly swayed by the supernatural messages, and couldn't help his belief in them. But, for Julie's sake, and to give Thorpe every possible chance, he had engaged Pennington Wise, and had invited him to stay at the Crane house while conducting his investigation.

So Wise came, and with him came his queer little assistant, the girl called Zizi.

There was ample room in the big city house, and the two were treated as honored guests.

Wise was alert, quick-witted and tactful, but Zizi was even more so. She made friends with the Cranes at once, and they all admired the odd, fascinating girl. Small of stature, dark of coloring, Zizi was not unlike a gypsy, and the mention of this brought about the tale of the gypsy's prophecy regarding Peter Boots.

"What an interesting story," the girl said, after hearing Benjamin Crane tell it. "It is wonderful how you dear people bear your loss so bravely."

"But it isn't really a loss," said Mrs. Crane, "you see, we have our boy with us continually."

It was only by desperate effort that Zizi kept from laughing, for of all fads or whims, spiritism seemed to her the worst and most foolish. But she was there on business, and part of her business was to gather all the information she could regarding this same spiritism, so she showed only deep interest and apparent sympathy with their beliefs.

"You do believe in these things, don't you?" Mrs. Crane asked, and, being thus confronted, Zizi had to answer directly.

"It's hard to say," she replied, "for, you see, I've had so little real experience. Practically none. But I'm eager to learn, and most interested in what you tell me."

"I'm a frank unbeliever," declared Pennington Wise. He had considered the matter and concluded it was better to state this fact and thereby rouse the others to defense.

"You wouldn't be, Mr. Wise," Benjamin Crane said, "if you'd had the experiences we're continually enjoying. You've read my book?"

"Yes, Mr. Crane, and an able, well written work it is. But you must number some among your friends who find difficulty in accepting it in just the way you do."

"Certainly, and though I do what I can to convince them, I think none the less of them for their honest unbelief. But with you right here in the house, Mr. Wise, it will, I'm sure, be an easy matter to make a convert of you."

"We'll see; at any rate, I'm ready to be converted if you can do it. Now, let's begin with that note your daughter received from—ah, shall I say from your son?"

"Of course, it was from my son. You may compare the writing with Peter's own—we've lots of his letters, and I think you'll be convinced it's no forgery."

"And it doesn't seem illogical to you," Wise went on, as he took the papers Crane handed to him, "that your son should materialize this paper, this note, and leave it for you, when, if he can do such things, he doesn't write a letter to his mother or to you?"

"From the average mortal's point of view there is much that seems illogical in spiritism," Crane said, easily, as if quite accustomed to answering such arguments; "we who believe, never question why or why not. We merely accept."

"Yes," said Mrs. Crane, "and when we are granted such wonderful boons as we are, it seems ungrateful and ungracious to ask for anything we do not get. When I hear my son's voice——"

"Do you recognize his voice?" asked Zizi.

"I can hardly say that, my dear, but we have heard Peter talk so often, through the medium, that it almost *seems* like his voice."

"And he told you that Mr. Thorpe was responsible for Mr. Blair's death?" Zizi went on, wanting a plain statement.

"Yes, he told us that."

"Then how can you have any doubt of it?"

"Spirits do not know everything. It is quite as likely for them to be misinformed as for earthly people to be. It may be that my boy doesn't know who killed Gilbert Blair, but has some reason to think it was Mr. Thorpe."

"Do you think it was?"

"I can't say that," Mrs. Crane looked very serious, "nor can I deny it. We are all so fond of Mr. Thorpe that we can scarcely bring ourselves to believe ill of him——"

"But if he is a criminal, we want to know it," her husband interrupted her. "Mr. Thorpe is engaged to my daughter, and if he is an innocent man, I want it made clear to the world. If not, then, of course, the engagement must be broken."

"He *is* an innocent man," Zizi said, quietly.

"Oh, you darling!" cried Julie, running across the room to embrace her. "How do you know?"

"By that letter," and Zizi pointed to the note from Peter, which she had been scrutinizing and comparing with some old letters of Peter's.

"You think it isn't from my brother?"

"I know it isn't. I've made a study of handwriting, and whoever wrote that wrote it in imitation of your brother's writing. I mean the writer was disguising his own hand and imitating your brother's."

"How can you tell? They are very much alike."

"That's just it. The salient points are imitated, the long terminal strokes, the peculiarities of the capitals, but the less conspicuous details, such as slant and spacing, are not so carefully copied. It is a forgery, and though well done enough to deceive the average observer, it would not deceive an expert."

"What a lot you know!" and Julie looked at the other girl in surprised admiration.

"'Course I do. It's my business to know things. Am I right about this, Penny Wise?"

"Yes," he said, smiling at her. "I thought you'd see it. Moreover, Mr. Crane, this note was written by a man, or by a person capable of deep, even venomous hatred. If, as may well be the case, it was written by the murderer of Mr. Blair, and with an intent to throw suspicion on Mr. Thorpe, then we must look for a criminal of great cleverness and of patience and perseverance in the workings of his nefarious plans. I mean a nature of inborn evil, capable of premeditated wrong. This murder of Gilbert Blair was no impulsive or suddenly brought about job. It was carefully planned and carefully carried out. If you will show me some of Mr. Thorpe's writing I will tell you if he forged this note."

"No, he did not," Wise asserted, after a study of a letter of Thorpe's, which they gave him; "we cannot say this note signed with your son's name was written by the criminal we're looking for, but we can be sure it was not written by McClellan Thorpe. You see, Mr. Crane, penmanship is a very exact science. Some one forged your son's writing, but he or she was utterly unable to omit the personal characteristics that are in every one's hand."

"And you can deduce character even from a forged hand?"

"Absolutely. It is those inevitable and unmistakable signs that make the individual writing a true mirror of character."

"But it is often impossible to determine the sex of a writer," Zizi informed them. "Frequently, to be sure, penmanship is undoubtedly that of a man or a woman, but sometimes it is not definitely evident. In this case, I think we have the work of a man, but I can't be sure."

"Who would do it, anyway?" queried Mrs. Crane.

"Any one interested in concealing the identity of the murderer and desiring to have Mr. Thorpe suspected. A clever person, because, knowing of Miss Crane's love of her brother and also knowing of your interest in the occult, it would doubtless seem to you a strong bit of evidence."

"It did," Benjamin Crane admitted, "at least, until you proved to us that it is not a note from my son at all. But you must remember, Mr. Wise, that we are in no way doubting my son's communications with us in other ways. If this is not from him, that does not cast doubt on other communications we have had from him. And, as he has repeatedly told us that Mr. Thorpe is responsible for Blair's death, I can only say that my boy may be mistaken, and I sincerely hope he is."

"Of course, he is," Julie cried. "Peter has sent us other messages that turned out to be untrue, but he was mistaken."

"You believe in the mediums, then?" asked Zizi, flashing her big dark eyes at the girl.

"Oh, I don't know. I didn't at first, and I was unwilling to, but I've heard so much and seen so much, and, of course, I can't help being influenced by Dad and Mother."

"Of course not," agreed Zizi. "It's all so interesting to me. I'm only afraid I'll become so absorbed in the spirits that I'll neglect the detective work."

"It may be they're interdependent," Wise observed.

"They are, I'm sure," said Julie. "You see, Mr. Wise, it's not only father and the medium that have told us things against Mr. Thorpe, but we have a friend who is an expert on the Ouija Board——"

Zizi rolled her eyes skyward.

"Oh," she groaned, "I thought you people were real honest-to-goodness Spiritists!"

"We are," defended Crane.

"Not if you fool with an Ouija Board!"

"But Carly, Miss Harper, can make it tell wonderful things," Julie went on, "things of which she really knows nothing."

"But the other person at the Board knows them?"

"Well, maybe; but they can't get Ouija to tell them without Miss Harper has her fingers on, too."

"And Ouija is against Mr. Thorpe?"

"Yes; at least it has said he was guilty, but, as you say, an Ouija Board means nothing."

"It means something, indeed, but not the thing it says."

"A brilliant remark, Zizi!" Wise smiled at her.

"But I mean just that, Penny. I'm getting a line on this thing, and I think that the criminal or the criminal's friends or accomplices are utilizing occult forces in their own behalf. I think, Miss Crane, the more messages you get telling you of Mr. Thorpe's guilt the more you may believe in his innocence!"

"Look out, Ziz, don't go too fast," Wise counseled her. "You've only begun this thing—there's a lot yet to be learned."

"I'll learn it, and I'm sure I'm headed in the right direction. And I'd like very much to see this Miss Harper. The Ouija witch! Has she told you to suspect Mr. Thorpe?"

"Don't put it that way," Julie begged. "Miss Harper is my dearest friend, and whatever she does with the Ouija Board is absolutely honest on her part, absolutely free from deceit."

"Then she's a unique case," declared Zizi. "Never has such a thing been known to science." Her smile robbed the words of invidious intent, and though Julie stood up for Carlotta's innocence, she had always wondered whether there was not some involuntary, even unconscious helping along done to the little board.

"Let's go to see her now," she suggested, and Wise agreeing, the two girls started off.

*   *   *   *   *

"This is Miss——?" Julie looked inquiringly at the girl she was about to introduce to Carlotta, remembering she didn't know her last name.

"Just Zizi," was the smiling reply, and the slim little dark hand was held out in greeting. "I'm so glad to know

you, Miss Harper. For, though I admit I don't believe in
Ouija, I am interested, and Miss Crane tells me you never
'push'."

"No, I never do that," Carlotta smiled, "but don't think
I believe in the thing, for I don't at all. It amuses me, and
it puzzled me, at first, but now I understand it, and it's
beginning to lose interest for me."

"Understand it?" Zizi looked bewildered. "You mean—
—"

"I mean I know what makes it work, why it tells the
truth, when it does tell the truth, and why it fibs when it
does fib."

Carly Harper's face was frank and honest; she had no
effect of mystery or clairvoyant power, and Zizi was
bewildered.

"I am indeed glad to know you!" she exclaimed, "will
you impart this knowledge to me, or is it a secret?"

"It's not a secret, perhaps it isn't knowledge, it's, after
all, only my own theory, or rather, discovery, based on
long and wide experience."

Zizi was enchanted.

"Oh, goody!" she cried, her black eyes dancing. "I'm
crazy to know just what you mean! Will you give me a
session with the board?"

"Will you promise not to push?"

"Of course, and, anyway, you'd know it if I did."

So Carly got the board, and the two sat at it, while
Julie looked on.

The usual routine followed, and at last the professed
spirit of Peter Crane was "present."

On being asked if Thorpe killed Gilbert Blair, the
Ouija Board promptly replied "No."

"Oh, Peter, the other day you said he did!" Carlotta
exclaimed, but again the Board flew to the corner where
"No" was printed.

Julie, watching closely, was sure neither of the girls in
any way cheated or helped things along. She was an

acute observer, and she was certain both the manipulators were strictly sincere.

"Well, then," Zizi said, her thin, dark fingers merely touching the little wooden heart, "who did?"

There was no reply. Motionless the board remained, and no persuasion would induce it to move.

Other subjects were brought up, questions were asked to which only Carlotta knew the answer, or to which only Zizi did, and they were answered, if not always definitely, at least in a general way. But when they returned to the question about Blair there was no response.

"Don't you know?" Carlotta demanded of Peter's "spirit," which obligingly announced its presence when requested.

But the board remained stationary, and they finally gave it up.

"All of which goes to prove my theory the true one," Carlotta declared, and then Zizi begged her to disclose her discoveries.

"Why, you see, it's this way," Carlotta began, "you get out of the Ouija Board exactly what you bring to it, no more, no less."

"Just what do you mean by that?"

"That nobody gets any information from the board unless it is already in his mind. When we ask questions, to which one of us knows the answer, that answer comes. Mind you, I don't mean that one of us pushes the board in the right direction, at least not consciously, but it is inevitable that the mind leaps ahead, and when a word is started we know, usually, what letter is coming next, and we receptively await it. You see, unless you hold your hands still purposely, the board is bound to move. Naturally it goes to the words you have in mind, and unless you purposely check it, the message is bound to come. If it is something I know and you don't, the board starts off, and as the words form, you don't stop them nor do I, yet we don't really force them, it's more as if we thought on the board. This is proved, to my mind, by the fact that if either party knows the answer, it always comes; if neither knows it, you can't get it. Usually the message is something that can't be verified anyway, and often the message is untrue. But people notice and remember the few times the truth is told, and quickly forget the other times. In no case are they messages from the dead. It is not Peter's spirit talking to us at all. It is merely our minds, subconsciously or not, that impel involuntary muscular action in the slightest degree, and our eagerness to get a certain word or phrase, brings it about. Tradition and habit ascribe the messages to the dead, and the universal desire to get such communications is responsible for the belief that they are such. Now, here's proof. Whenever I have asked the Board who killed Gilbert it has responded with the name of the person whom my companion thought guilty. I have no idea who is the criminal, neither, I take it, has Zizi; consequently, as we are both open-minded and waiting for the answer, we get nothing."

"Right," and Zizi nodded her head. "People fool themselves into believing they get information from Ouija. But, if they were honest, they would have to admit that never has it told a truth that was not known to at least one person present. Of course, I except coincidences, which must happen occasionally."

"But," objected Julie, "then why will it work so much better when Carly has her hands on?"

"Just because I'm impassive," Carlotta said, "and sit quietly while the other one gets the message she wants. Without effort the message desired comes, merely because nobody stops it."

"Then," said Julie, "none of the help we get from Ouija means anything at all?"

"No, and it isn't help," said Zizi.

CHAPTER 13: "LABRADOR LUCK"

Kit Shelby's play was a wonderful success. Though a motion picture, it was one of the finest ever produced, and no expense had been spared to make it the sensation of the season. It was called "Labrador Luck."

The Crane family attended the opening night, as, indeed, all Shelby's friends did, and the verdict was unanimous that never had such a beautiful and finished play been screened. The scenes of ice-bound Labrador were picturesque and fascinating, while the plot was ingenious and thrills plentiful. The audience applauded continuously, for so real was the acting that it seemed as if the performers were actually there.

Benjamin Crane had helped Shelby finance the production, and he realized at once that he would get his money back with interest.

"It's a gold mine, boy!" he said to Shelby, as they were all at the Crane home afterward, "and it must be made into a spoken drama. There's scope for a great play in that plot."

"Marvelous plot," commented Pennington Wise. "All your own, Mr. Shelby?"

"Yes," Kit replied, with frank pride; "it did turn out well, didn't it?"

"And you're going to make a book of it, too, aren't you?" asked Julie.

"Yes, a book, and a serial story and, oh, I'm going to do lots of things with it!"

"Grand opera, maybe!" chaffed Julie.

"Why not?" said Shelby, seriously. "Slighter plots than that have been put into grand opera. It may yet come about."

Without undue conceit Shelby was quite conscious of his great success, and as he walked home with Carlotta from the Crane house, he begged her to consent to his repeated proposals of marriage.

"This thing will make me rich, dear," he said, "and while that sounds mercenary, it does make me glad to have a fortune to offer you."

"But I don't love you, Kit," and Carlotta smiled carelessly at him.

"You will, Carly. You'll have to, 'cause I love you so. Oh, sweetheart, I love you just desperately— I must have you, my little girl, I must!"

"Now, Kit, you wouldn't want a wife who didn't care for you as a woman ought to care for the man she marries. Truly, my heart is still Peter's. I sometimes think I'll never marry, his memory is so vivid and so dear to me."

"Weren't you beginning to care for Blair?"

"N-no; not that way. Of course I was fond of Gilbert, and I'm fond of you, but there's always the thought of Peter between us."

"But, Carly, there's no one you care more for than for me, is there?"

"No, I'm sure of that."

"Then say yes, darling. Even though you won't marry me quite yet, let's be engaged, and truly you'll soon learn to love me. I'll make you!"

But Carlotta wouldn't consent, and Shelby had to be content with her promise to think about it.

"Kit," she said, suddenly, "are those queer detectives going to find out who killed Gilbert?"

"Oh, I suppose they'll fasten it on Mac. Poor chap, to think of his being in jail while we're having all this excitement over my play. But I don't see any other direction for Wise to look. What a funny little thing that Zizi is."

"Yes, but I like her a lot. And she's nobody's fool! Her black eyes take in everything, whether she remarks on it or not. You should have seen her watch you to-night."

"When?"

"At the Cranes', when you were talking about the play."

"She's dramatic herself. She ought to be in the Moving Pictures!"

"Yes, she'd be a film queen at once."

* * * * *

Zizi must have had something of the same idea in her own mind, for the next day she went to see Shelby at his office and asked him if he could give her a chance at film work.

"But you're a detective," Shelby said, amusedly, "what would Mr. Wise do without you?"

"He'd get along all right," Zizi said earnestly. "He's willing I should have a try at a screen career, if you'll take me on."

"I'm not sure I could use you," Shelby returned, "at least not at present. If I do another picture I'll try you out in it."

"Oh, you are going to do another, aren't you?"

"Probably, but not until I've exhausted all the different possibilities of this one."

Zizi showed her disappointment at the failure of her plan, but, after some further talk on general subjects, she went back to the Cranes'.

"Well, Ziz," Wise said to her, as they discussed the case alone, "we're not making our usual rapid headway this time. Rather baffling, isn't it?"

"Everything seems to point to Thorpe, except that I can't think he had motive enough. That foolish jealousy of the plans and suspicion of Blair's stealing his ideas isn't enough to make him commit murder."

"I don't think he did do it, but I can't agree with you that it wasn't a big enough motive. You don't know how the artistic temperament resents anything like that. Nor how it imagines and exaggerates the least hint of it. I think his motive is the strongest point against Thorpe. Who else had any motive at all?"

"That's what we have to find out. And we're going to do it. And, I say, Penny, I want to go to see that medium person the Cranes are so fond of."

"Think she'll help you?"

"Yes, though not by her spiritism. But I suspect she's one big fraud, and I want to be sure."

"Come along, then. No time like the present. Mr. Crane can arrange a session for us."

To Madame Parlato's they went, and soon had the pleasure of seeing that lady in one of her trances.

The room was dimly lighted but not in total darkness. After a silence a faint, low-pitched voice said, "I am here."

"Are you Peter Crane?" asked Zizi, who chose to be spokesman.

"Yes."

"Will you talk to us?"

"Yes, for a short time only."

"Very well, then tell us who killed Gilbert Blair."

"His friend, McClellan Thorpe. Good-by."

"Wait a minute. I own up to being skeptical, is it too much to ask for some proof of your identity, Peter Crane? Will you, can you give some material proof?"

"It is not easy."

"I'm sorry for that, but, oh, I do so want to be convinced. And I can't, unless I have something tangible to take away with me. Do give me something."

There was a silence, and then, apparently from nowhere, a handkerchief fluttered through the air and fell at Zizi's feet.

Amazed, the girl picked it up, and though she could not see it distinctly, she discovered it was a large one, evidently a man's.

Suddenly the medium sat up straight, came out of her trance, and putting on the lights, said, eagerly, "Did you get any message?"

"I should say I did!" Zizi returned, "and a material proof, too. Look!"

"Wonderful!" exclaimed Madame Parlato, as she looked at the white square of linen. "Initialed, too."

"Yes, P. C.," and Zizi scrutinized the embroidery.

Pennington Wise expressed a polite admiration for the medium who could bring about such marvelous results, and the *seance* over, the two departed, Zizi carrying the handkerchief in her bag.

"One of a set of Peter's," Wise said, confidently.

"Of course. Julie or Mrs. Crane will recognize it. Funny, how she thought a crude performance like that would convince us!"

"Mighty well done though."

"Pooh, in a darkened room one can do anything."

"Well, where did she get the handkerchief?"

"Dunno, yet. Maybe the Cranes left it there by chance."

"Oh, no, that won't do. Guess again."

"I think I could if I tried. But we'll see what the family say about it."

Both Mrs. Crane and Julie declared the handkerchief to be one of Peter's own, and, moreover, that it was one of a set Carlotta had embroidered for him just before he went to Labrador. And he had taken the whole dozen with him, of that they were both sure. It had been Carly's parting gift, and Peter had been delighted with it.

"It's too wonderful!" Julie said, amazed. "Now, how do you explain it, Zizi? We know this to be Peter's own handkerchief. We know he took it to Labrador with him. How did it get back here? How get into Madame Parlato's possession? And how appear to you, out of nothingness?"

"Yes," said Benjamin Crane, smiling happily, "answer those questions satisfactorily, or else admit that it is real materialization!"

Wise looked a little nonplused. Positive though he was of the medium's trickery, he could not tell Mr. Crane exactly how it had come about. Materialization was easy enough for a charlatan, but, as had been said, where could she get the handkerchief to do the trick with?

Convinced of the Cranes' honesty, of course, Wise couldn't doubt that Peter had taken all the handkerchiefs with him. His luggage had never been sent home, therefore how did the handkerchief get to New York, and more especially how did it get to Madame Parlato?

"I can't explain it yet," Wise said, frankly, "but I'll find out all about it. To you, Mr. Crane, it seems additional proof of your son's communication through that medium. To me it is additional and very strong proof of her fraud. Now, we'll leave it at that for the present, but I promise to explain it to you soon."

"All right, Mr. Wise, you'll not be offended, I trust, if I say I don't believe you can make good your word. But I'm not surprised at your attitude. Some minds are almost incapable of belief in the occult, and will accept the most absurd and far-fetched explanations rather than the simple and plausible one of spirit communication. I can't understand such a mental attitude, but I've met so many like you that I'm obliged to recognize its existence."

"Oh, Mr. Wise," Mrs. Crane said, "it does seem so strange that a clear-headed, deep-thinking man like yourself prefers to believe that Madame Parlato could get Peter's handkerchief and could produce it so mysteriously for you rather than the rational belief that Peter sent it himself."

Zizi looked at the speaker with kindly eyes.

"Dear Mrs. Crane," she said, "what will hurt me most when we expose that medium's fraud is the fact of your disappointment."

"Don't worry about that," smiled Benjamin Crane, "you haven't exposed her yet! Meantime, I shall incorporate this experience of the handkerchief in my next book."

"Oh, don't!" cried Zizi, involuntarily. "You'll make yourself a laughing-stock——"

She paused, unwilling to hurt his feelings.

But so assured of his beliefs was Benjamin Crane that he shook his head and said:

"No fear of that, child. I'll take all risks. Have you any idea how my book has been received? It's just gone into another big edition, and my publishers are clamoring for my second book, which is nearly finished. But to return to the case of McClellan Thorpe. Did Peter tell you——"

"Yes," Wise said, "according to Madame Parlato, the spirit of your son said that Thorpe is the criminal, and it was as proof of identity that Zizi received the handkerchief."

"Fine," said Crane, nodding his satisfaction, "I think I'll use that *seance* for the finale of my book, and get it in press at once."

"Do, dear," said his wife, "as far as the handkerchief is concerned. But don't put in the book that Mac killed Gilbert."

"Oh, no, certainly not. In the first place, we're all agreed that though Peter believes that, it is a mistake on his part; that is, it may be a mistake. Don't let it influence you too much, Mr. Wise."

Penny Wise laughed outright. He couldn't help it.

"No, sir," he promised, "I won't!"

"But have you any other suspect?"

"I'd rather not answer that question quite yet, Mr. Crane."

"All right, take your own time. I've confidence you'll do all you can, but my hopes of your success are dwindling."

"Don't feel that way, on the contrary, I'm beginning to see at least a way to look for another suspect."

"Look hard, then. For I want to get Mac cleared as soon as it can be brought about."

"We'll hope to do that. I'm going over to the Studios now, and I've a notion I'll discover something."

Accompanied by Zizi, Wise went to the home that Blair and Thorpe had occupied, and which was now in charge of the police.

The detective set himself to the task of looking over old letters and papers in hope of finding out some secret of the dead man's past.

Zizi flitted about the rooms, looking for nothing in particular, and everything in general.

"I've sized up his medicines," she said, coming from Blair's bedroom into the studio where Wise sat at the desk.

"His cough syrup hasn't been touched lately. The dried up stickiness of the cork shows that. And one or two other bottles are in the same condition. But in the waste basket in his bedroom I found this."

She held up an empty bottle that was labeled soda mints.

"There's a new full bottle in the medicine chest," she went on, "and as this was in the basket, mayn't it be that he took the last ones, and——"

"And they were poisoned!"

"One of them was. See, somebody had put a poisoned one in among the others."

"That leads back to Thorpe, who else could do that?"

"And we don't know that anybody did, only it might have been."

"Can you smell any prussic acid in the vial?"

"No," and Zizi sniffed at it, "I seem to think I do, but I daresay it's my vivid imagination. Do you suppose a chemist could discern any?"

"Probably not, but we might make a try at it. Pretty slim clue, anyway, Ziz."

"I know it, but I have a hunch it's the real thing. You see, Blair was in the habit of taking these things——"

"How do you know?"

"Carlotta Harper told me. I've quizzed her a lot about Mr. Blair's personal habits, and he always carried soda mints in his pocket, and took one now and then. So, as there was no soda mint bottle found in his pockets, and this was in the basket, it's a logical deduction that he finished this bottle that night that he died. And they all think the poison was given to him through some simple trick, so why not this?"

"It may be. It very likely is. But where does it get us?"

"Dunno yet. But, say it was done that way, it needn't have been done here. Maybe the murderer put a poisoned mint in the bottle when they were somewhere together."

"How could he?"

"Oh, lots of ways. Say Blair had his coat off, playing golf or billiards, or——"

"He'd carry such a bottle in his waistcoat pocket, I think."

"Well, it's all surmise. The thing to do is to begin from the other end. Who had a motive?"

"That's what I'm trying to trace. Nothing doing as yet. Hello, here's that old letter from Joshua, the guide. Look at it! It is in a small, cramped hand, and you know the one purporting to be from him later was in a big, sprawly hand. Somebody faked that letter!"

"Well, there's something to work on, then."

"But maybe Thorpe did it."

"Not he. Why should he? He had nothing to do with that Labrador trip."

"What was the letter about, the other Joshua letter?"

"Advising him not to try to bring Peter Crane's body down to New York, or to postpone the matter, or something like that."

"Queer business, that. Why should anybody want to fake a letter like that?"

"I don't believe anybody did. More likely some one else wrote for the guide. They're an ignorant lot, and writing is an unwelcome task to them."

They were still looking at the guide's letter when Shelby came in.

"I heard you were here," he said, "and thought it would be a good time to come around. I want to see if there's anything in Blair's papers that would help to turn suspicion away from Mac Thorpe. I don't believe that man did it, and I wish we could free him."

"That's what we're after," and Wise made room for Shelby to sit beside him at Blair's desk.

But though they made systematic search of all letters they found none other than friendly. There were some from his mother and sister, pathetic ones, telling of their ill health, for both were invalids.

They had not come East on learning of Blair's death, for they could not well stand the trip, and, too, there was no real reason for their coming. After the police investigation was over Blair's effects were to be sent to them, but for the present everything remained as it was found at his death.

"Let me help you, if I can," Shelby went on to Wise. "You know Blair and I were chums. Poor Gilbert, and Peter Boots, too, both gone, and both by such tragic means. I don't know which death was the worse."

Zizi showed him the small bottle she had found, and asked his opinion of her theory about it.

"What an ingenious notion," Shelby exclaimed; "yes, it might be the truth, of course, but a dozen other ways might have been used either."

"Such as what?" asked Wise, "it's always a help to talk these things over."

"Well, granting that some one administered poison to Blair, secretly, mightn't he have put it in anything that Blair was about to eat or drink?"

"Not this poison," objected Wise. "It acts too quickly. Whatever plan was adopted, it was some scheme by which Blair would take the poison unknowingly, but naturally. As Zizi says, if it had been put in some one of his bottles of medicine, he must take it, sooner or later."

"Yes; well, then say it was put in a cigarette, no that's foolish; why, hang it all, Wise, don't you see there's no plausible theory except that some one put it in a drink

Blair took just before going to bed, or even after he was in bed."

"Where's the glass, then?"

"That's just the point. What's the answer, except that Thorpe washed it and put it away? Of course, Blair would take a drink Thorpe offered him."

"Also, he might have taken a soda mint just as he went to bed or after," said Zizi.

"Yes," agreed Shelby, thoughtfully. "He might have done so, but could one introduce poison into one of those things? They're quite hard, you know."

"Yes, it could be done," Wise declared. "I've heard of such a thing before. The little pellet could be soaked in the poison——"

"That would make it taste, and he wouldn't swallow it," Shelby said.

"True. Well, I think, with a hypodermic needle, the poison could be got into the mint."

"Maybe, but I doubt it. However, I don't know much about such things. You're doubtless experienced."

"Yes, I've had a lot of poison cases. And, if we give up all thought of the soda mint, it does come back to a drink of some sort mixed by Thorpe."

"Or Blair might have mixed his own drink, and Thorpe added the poison, unnoticed."

"But I want to get away from Thorpe," Zizi said, her eyes anxious and worried.

"So do we all," returned Shelby gravely. "But where can we look?"

"Where, indeed?" echoed Penny Wise.

CHAPTER 14: A PROPHECY FULFILLED

Among the passengers disembarking from a steamer at a Brooklyn pier was a tall, gaunt man, who walked with a slight limp.

He was alone, and though he nodded pleasantly to one or two of his fellow passengers, he walked by himself, and all details of landing being over, he took a taxicab to a hotel restaurant, glad to eat a luncheon more to his taste than the ship's fare had been.

He bought several New York papers, and soon became so absorbed in their contents that his carefully selected food might have been dust and ashes for all he knew.

Staring at an advertisement, he called a waiter.

"Send out and get me that book," he said, "as quick as you can."

"Yes, sir," returned the man, "it's right here, sir, on the news-stand. Get it in a minute, sir."

And in about a minute Peter Boots sat, almost unable to believe his own eyes, as he scanned the chapter headings of his father's book, detailing the death and the subsequent experiences of him who sat and stared at the pages.

He looked at the frontispiece, a portrait of himself, but bearing little resemblance to his present appearance. For, where the pictured face showed a firm, well-molded chin, the living man wore a brown beard, trimmed Vandyke fashion, and where the expression on the portrait showed a merry, carefree smile, the real face was graven with deep lines that told of severe experiences of some sort.

But the real face grinned a little at the picture, and broke into a wider smile at some sentences read at random as the pages were hastily turned, and then as further developments appeared, the blue eyes showed a look of puzzled wonder, quickly followed by horror and despair.

Peter closed the book and laid it aside, and finished his luncheon in a daze.

One thing stood forth in his mind. He must take time to think—think deeply, carefully, before he did anything. He must get away by himself and meet this strange, new emergency that had come to him.

What to do, how to conduct himself, these were questions of gravest import, and not to be lightly settled.

He thought quickly, and concluded that for a secure hiding-place a man could do no better than choose a big city hotel.

Finishing his meal he went to the desk and asked for a room, registering as John Harrison, which was the name by which he had been known on the ship that had brought him to port.

Once behind the locked door of his room he threw himself into an armchair and devoured the book he had bought.

Rapidly he flew through it; then went over it again, more slowly, until Peter Boots was familiar with every chapter of the book that his father had written in his memory.

Memory! And he wasn't dead!

The book, he saw, had gone through a large number of editions, wherefore, many people had read the tale of his tragic fate in the Labrador wild, and of his recrudescence and communications with his parents, and now, here he was reading it himself.

It is not easy to realize how strange it must seem to read not only one's own death notices but the accounts of one's return to earth in spirit form, and to be informed of the astonishing things one said and did through the kind offices of a professional medium!

A medium! Madame Parlato! And she "got in touch" with him! She succeeded in getting messages from him— and materializations!

Peter's chicory blue eyes nearly popped out of his head when he read of the "materialization" of his tobacco pouch.

"Jolly glad I know where it is," he thought; "I've missed the thing, but how did it waft itself to a professional medium! Bah! the stuff makes me sick!

"But Dad wrote it! Dad—my father! And mother's in the game! Got to read the book all over again."

And again he delved into the volume, seeming unable to take in the appalling fact of what had been done.

"They believe it!" he said at last, reaching the final page for the third time; "they believe it from the bottom of their blessed souls!

"Who is that medium person? Where'd she get the dope to fool the old folks? Let me at her! I'll give her what for! Messages to mother from her departed son! 'Do not grieve for me,' 'I am happy over here,' Oh, for the love o' Mike! what *am* I going to do first?"

Followed a long time of thought. At first, chaotic, wondering, uncertain, then focussing and crystallizing into two definite ideas.

One, the astonishing but undeniable fact of his father's belief and sincerity, the other, what would happen if that belief and sincerity were suddenly stultified.

"Good Lord!" he summed up, "when I appear on the scene that medium will get the jolt of her sweet young life— I assume she's young still, and Dad——

"H'm, where will he get off?"

That gave him pause. For Benjamin Crane to have written such a book as this, for it to have achieved such a phenomenal success and popularity, for it to have been the means, as it doubtless was, of converting thousands to a belief in Spiritism, then, for the whole thing to be overturned by the reappearance in the flesh of the man supposed dead, would mean a cataclysm unparalleled in literary history.

And his father? The dear old man, happy in his communications from his dead son, how would he be pleased to learn that they were not from his dead son at all, but the faked drivel of a fraudulent medium?

It was a moil, indeed.

Peter Crane had come home incognito, because he doubted the wisdom of a sudden shock to his parents. Unable to send or get news, and making his voyage home at the first possible opportunity, he had intended to learn how matters stood before making his appearance.

He had intended telephoning Blair and Shelby, and if they said all was well at home he would go there at once. But if there had been illness or death he would use care and tact in making his presence known.

For Peter Boots had had no word of, or from his people for half a year—all the long Labrador winter he had lived in ignorance of their welfare and had suffered to the limit, both mentally and physically.

And he had thought they would probably assume his death—as, by reason of this astonishing book he now knew they had done—and, what was he to do about it?

Impulse would have sent him flying home—home to his mother, Dad and Julie, and—and dear little Carly.

But—when he thought of the possibility of his reappearance being the means of making his father's name a by-word of ridicule, of heaping on the old man's fame obloquy and derision, of shocking his mother, perhaps fatally, or at least into a nervous prostration, he was unable to shape a course.

Could he tell Carly first? He glanced at a telephone book at his elbow.

No, that would never do. To hear his voice on the telephone would throw her into a convulsion. He didn't believe she stood for that spirit foolishness, but if, by any chance, she had been won over, his voice would surely give her some sort of a shock.

The boys, then. Yes, that was the only thing. He must see them, but he must telephone first and learn their whereabouts.

He could, he concluded, call in a disguised voice, and get a line on things anyhow.

So, still in a haze of doubt and uncertainty, he looked up the number and called Shelby.

As he rather expected, Shelby was not at his home, but the person who answered could give no directions save to say that Mr. Shelby would probably be home by six o'clock, and would he leave a message?

"No," returned Peter shortly, and hung up.

Getting next the number of the Leonardo Studios, he asked for Gilbert Blair.

"W-what—who?" came a stammering response.

"Mr. Blair—Mr. Gilbert Blair," repeated Peter.

"Why—why, he's dead—Mr. Blair's dead."

"No! When did he die?"

"Coupla months ago. Murdered."

"What!"

"Yep, murdered."

Peter hung up the receiver from sheer inability to do anything else.

Of course it couldn't be true. Blair couldn't have been murdered, and he must have misunderstood that last word. But his arm seemed paralyzed when he tried again to take hold of the telephone.

He sank back in his chair and tried to think.

His subconscious mind told him that he had not misunderstood—that Gilbert was murdered. He knew he had heard the word correctly, and people do not make such statements unless they are true.

His thoughts gradually untangled themselves and he began to grapple with the most important problems.

It was clear that he must learn what had happened in his absence. He wanted to get hold of Shelby and ask about Blair. He wanted to go right over to Blair's place—

but if—if *it* had occurred two months ago there was small use going there now.

Also, he must preserve his incognito for the present, at least. His return would be blazoned in the papers as soon as it was known, and the effect on his father's reputation would be most disastrous.

He must learn more facts—the facts he had already discovered were so amazing, what else might not be in store for him?

Concentrating on the subject of Blair's death he concluded his best course would be to get a file of newspapers covering the past two months and read about it.

In a big newspaper office he accomplished this, and spent the rest of the afternoon reading up the case.

Of late the subject was not a principal one in the papers.

McClellan Thorpe was in prison, awaiting his trial, and the police, while still on the job, were not over aggressive.

Pennington Wise was not mentioned, so Peter had no means of knowing that that astute person was connected with the matter.

But the news of Thorpe's arrest struck Peter a new blow. While not as chummy with Thorpe as with Shelby and Blair, Peter had always liked him and found it difficult to believe him guilty of Blair's death.

Back to his hotel went the man registered as John Harrison, and, going to the restaurant for dinner, he ate and enjoyed a hearty meal.

After all, strange and weird as was the news he had heard, his parents were alive and well—and, strangest of all, they were not grieving at his death.

He was relieved at this, and yet, he was, in an inexplicable way, disappointed. It *is* a blow in the face to learn that your loved ones are quite reconciled to your death because, forsooth, they get fool messages from you through the services of a fool medium!

Peter's ire rose, and he was all for going to his father's house at once, and then, back came the thought, how could he put that dear old man to the blush for having written that preposterous book?

From the papers, too, Peter had learned of the furor the book had made, of the great notoriety and popularity that had come to Benjamin Crane from its publication, of the enormous sales it had had, and was still having, and of the satisfaction and happiness the whole thing had brought to both Mr. and Mrs. Crane.

So, stifling his longing to go home and to see his people, Peter decided to sleep over it before taking any definite steps.

He had small fear of recognition. Nobody in New York believed him alive, or had any thought of looking for him. His present appearance was so different from the portrait in the book that, after he had changed his looks still further by a different brushing of his hair, he felt there was no trace of likeness left save perhaps his blue eyes. And only one who knew him well would notice his eyes, and he had no expectation of running up against one who knew him well.

So, after dinner, he sat for a time in the hotel lobby, not wishing to mingle with his fellow men, yet not wishing to seem peculiar by reason of his evading notice.

Worn with the succession of shocks that had come to him, and weary of meeting the big problems and situations, he thought of diversion.

"Any good plays on?" he asked the news-stand girl, and his winning smile brought a chatty response.

"Plays—yes. Nothing corking, though. But say, have you seen the big movie?"

"No; what is it?"

"'Labrador Luck,' oh, say, it's a peach! Go to it!"

"Where?" and Peter stopped himself just in time from exclaiming, "Labrador anything would interest me!"

"Over in N'York. Hop into the sub and you're there."

Peter hopped into the sub and shortly he was there.

"Labrador Luck," he read from the big posters. "Monster production of the Tophole Producing Company. Thrilling scenes, thrilling plot, thrilling drama."

There was more detail as to the names of the Film Queen who was starred, and the Film King who supported her, but without stopping to read them Peter bought a ticket and went in.

The picture was under way, and as he sank into his seat he saw on the screen the familiar scenes of the Labrador wild.

Not quite true to nature were they, this Peter recognized at once, but he knew they were taken in a studio, not in Labrador itself, and he had only admiration for the cleverness with which they were done.

With a little sigh of pleasure he gave himself up to a positive enjoyment of the landscape, and, as the story went on, he was conscious of a vaguely familiar strain running through it.

Suddenly a scene was flashed on, and an episode occurred which was one of his own invention.

"Why," he smiled, "that's my very idea! Now how'd they get that? Oh, I know, of course, such things often occur to various minds without collusion, but it's sort of queer. If he follows up that lead, it will be awful queer!"

The lead was followed up, and, a bit bewildered, Peter sat gazing while the whole story was unrolled.

Greatly changed it was, greatly elaborated; the main plot side-tracked by a counter-plot; the number of characters multiplied by a score; yet, the mystery interest, the suspense element, the very backbone of the piece was the plot he and Blair had worked out while up in the Labrador wild.

"Labrador Luck!" he mused. "Fine name for it, too. The 'Luck' being that old heirloom—just as I planned it. Wonder how it all came about?"

Then he realized how long he'd been away from Blair. How Blair, doubtless, supposed him dead, and, most naturally, the boy had gone on with the story, and here was the splendid result.

He sat through the thing enthralled, and when the finale came, so exactly as he had planned that smashing great scene, he could have yelled his applause. But he didn't, he simply sat still in glad anticipation of seeing it all over again.

But he was disappointed. It was not a continuous performance—the long play was a whole evening's entertainment, and opening and closing hours were like those of a regular theater.

So Peter determined to come the next night to see it again, and to see the first part that he had missed.

"Great old play," he thought, delightedly. "Wonder if Blair put it on before he died, or if it's posthumous."

He picked up a stray program as he left the place—he had had none before—and put it in his pocket to look over at home.

"At least, I'm not suffering from lack of interests or diversion," he said, "but, by Jingo, I've just thought of it! What about money!

"I've enough to hang out at that hotel about a week and that's all. I'll have to tell Dad I'm here, or get a job or rob a bank. And what can I do to turn an honest penny? And I can't go to work under an assumed name! Oh, hang it all, I've got to come to life! Much as I love Dad and much as I want to save him from all ridicule and disaster about that abominable book, I've simply got to live my own life!

"But I won't decide till my cash gets lower than it is now. I'll go a bit further in my investigations and then we'll see about it."

Comfortably seated in his room he drew out the program to look over.

To his unbounded amazement he learned from the title page that the author of the play and also the producer, or, at least, the president of the producing company was—Christopher Shelby!

"Kit! Good old top!" he cried aloud.

"Oh, I must see him," he thought, "I just must see him! So Kit wrote the thing—well, I suppose he and Blair did it together— I recognize Kit's hand more especially in the producing element—and then, old Gilbert, bless him, was killed, and Kit went ahead alone— I can't think Mac Thorpe did for Gil—oh, I must see *somebody* or I'll go crazy!"

And because he was afraid to trust himself to keep away from the telephone any longer, Peter Boots went to bed.

The night brought counsel.

Clarifying his thoughts, Peter tried first to see where his duty lay.

To his parents, first of all, he decided, for he was a devoted son, and all his life he had loved and revered both father and mother more than most boys do. Julie, too, but, so far he had no reason to think she had any special claim on him.

Well, then, what did his duty to his parents dictate?

Common sense said that they would far rather have their son with them alive than to rest secure in the success of the book his father had written.

But the book itself was, to his mind, quite outside the pale of common sense, and could not be judged by any such standards.

Certain pages, special paragraphs in that book, stood out in his mind, and he knew that never had there been such a fiasco as would ensue if the long lost and deeply mourned hero of it should return! His return in the spirit was so gloatingly related, so triumphantly averred, that his return in the flesh would be a terrific anti-climax.

He remembered the gypsy's prophecy—how it had come true!

But the return, foretold by the second gypsy, was now verified in the flesh and put to naught all the fake returns narrated in the book.

Much stress was laid, in his father's story, on the spiritual return being what the gypsy meant. Now, Peter had proved that that prophecy meant, if it meant anything at all, his return in the flesh.

Anyway, here he was, very much alive, and very uncertain what to do with his live self.

Should he go away, out West, or to some distant place and start life anew, under an assumed name, and leave his father to his delusion? Was that his duty?

He was not necessary to his parents, either as a help to their support or as a comfort to their hearts.

He did not do them the injustice to think that they had never mourned for him, or that they had not missed him in the home. All this was fully and beautifully set forth in the book.

But they had been compensated by the comfort and enjoyment afforded them by their *seances*, and by the messages they continually received from him!

And he could see no way, try as he would, that he could inform them of his return without causing them dismay and distress.

For if they knew him to be alive he must take again his old place in the home—and then what would his father be?

A laughing-stock, a crushed and crestfallen victim of the most despicable sort of fraud!

It would never do. He couldn't bring positive trouble into his father's life on the off chance of removing a sorrow, which, though real, was softened and solaced by the very fraud that he would expose.

No; the more he thought the more he saw his duty was to eliminate himself for all time from his home and friends.

And Carly?

He tried not to think about her, for his duty must be his paramount consideration. He would wait a day or so, and then disappear again, and forever.

CHAPTER 15: AN INTERVIEW

"Well, Mr. Douglas, what can I do for you?"

Benjamin Crane spoke cordially, and smiled genially at the young man who had called on him in his home.

"You can turn me down, sir, if you like, or, if you'll be so kind, you can give me a few details of these strange experiences of yours in occult matters."

"Are you a reporter?"

"I am, but also I want to be something more than that. And in this case I want to write up these things for a special article, and a personal interview would help a lot."

"Well, my boy, you impress me pleasantly, and, as I like nothing better than to talk on my favorite subject, I'll give you a fifteen-minute chat. More than that I cannot spare time for."

"Then let's confine our talk to the phase that interests me most. I can get your beliefs and experiences from your book, you know. And your personality," Douglas gave him a humorously appraising glance, "I am gathering as we go along. First, will you tell me your attitude, mental and spiritual, regarding the loss of your son? I mean, though I fear I put it crudely, are you entirely reconciled to his death because of the comfort you receive from his—er—communications and all that?"

"A difficult question to answer," Crane paused a moment, "but I think I may say yes. I bow to the will of a Higher Power in the death of my son, and I am grateful to that same Higher Power for the comfort that is mine in the communion I have with my boy."

"Then you do not really grieve over his loss?"

"Not now—no. At first, of course, both his mother and I were crushed, but when he came to us, in the spirit, we took heart, and now we are perfectly satisfied—more than satisfied to accept our life conditions just as they are."

"You have frequent communication with the spirit of your departed son?"

"Almost daily."

"With the same medium always?"

"Nowadays, yes. I tried various ones, but I rely on Madame Parlato. She has had the greatest success, and now can readily get into communication with my son at almost any time."

"Excuse me, Mr. Crane, if I am indiscreet, but have you never felt that she might be—not entirely—honest?"

Benjamin Crane smiled benignly. "Don't hesitate to put your doubt into words. I am quite ready to answer that question. I have no doubts of any sort concerning the medium's honesty, sincerity and genuineness. I have no doubt that the communications she obtains are really from my son Peter. That his spirit speaks to me through her. This has been proved to me in many ways, but a far greater proof is the conviction in my soul of the reality of it all. My wife believes as implicitly as I do, and no amount of scoffing from outsiders can in any way shake our faith."

"You have had material proofs?"

"Yes; here is a letter from my son himself. Here is a tobacco pouch that I know was his. Here is his handkerchief."

With a calm pride Benjamin Crane took these articles from a table drawer and showed them.

Douglas was deeply impressed, examined the articles and watched Crane as he returned them to the drawer.

"You see," said Crane, "it is not only difficult but impossible to account for those things except by supernatural explanation, so why refuse the logical truth?"

"That's so. And, I understand now, why you are so happy in your beliefs, for it all gives your life a continual and absorbing interest. You are writing another book, are you not?"

"Yes; it contains the detailed account of my *seances*, and will, I trust, prove an additional source of information and education on the great subject of survival."

"And your daughter? Does she, too, subscribe to all your theories?"

"Almost entirely. She is not so absorbed in the subject as Mrs. Crane and myself, but she has become persuaded of many truths."

"And now, my time is nearly up, may I ask you a word regarding the Blair case. Do you think McClellan Thorpe is the guilty man?"

"No! a thousand times no! I am trying by every means in my power to prove that he isn't. I hope to succeed, too. But we mustn't go into that subject, as I have an important appointment to keep. Come to see me again, Mr. Douglas, if you like. I'm not unaccustomed to such calls, and I'll be glad to see you again. By appointment, though, for I'm a busy man."

Tom Douglas went back, over to Brooklyn, and, going to a hotel, asked for one John Harrison.

In a short time Peter Boots was eagerly listening to the report of the messenger he had sent to his father.

"I learned a lot, Mr. Harrison," the visitor began. "I think I can give you quite a bit of the local color you need for your novel."

"Not so much local color as mental attitude," Peter returned. "You see, in writing a psychological novel the author has to be careful of shades of feeling in his delineation of the characters. And as this Mr. Crane seemed to be just the type I want to study, I'm glad to have you tell me all the things he said, as nearly as you can recollect his own language."

"Yes, I know. And I was mighty interested on my own account, too."

"He was willing you should write an article about him?"

"Oh, yes, and asked me to come again."

"Go on, tell me all he said—how he looked and acted and everything that happened."

And so the young reporter and free-lance writer told Peter Boots all about his father, under the impression that he was talking to one who had never seen Benjamin Crane.

"He's a wonderful man, Mr. Harrison," the other said, enthusiastically. "He must be fifty-five at least, maybe more, but he's so alert and quick-witted, and so full of his subject, that he seems a much younger man."

"And he seems happy?"

"Happy! I should say so! Perfectly reconciled to his son's death, because of these communications he gets from him! I say, Mr. Harrison, I can't stand for it! It gets me to see how that man is gulled, and he such a clear-headed, sane sort! Had proofs, too—all sorts of things. Do you believe it, Mr. Harrison? Do you believe that the spirit of Mr. Crane's dead son talks to him through a medium?"

"I do not," said Peter Crane, endeavoring not to speak too emphatically. "I didn't want you to get that interview in the interests of Spiritism at all, but to tell me of the condition, mentally and physically, of Mr. Crane."

"Yes, I know. Well, the old guy is O.K. physically, fit as a fiddle. And sound mentally, you bet, except that he's nutty on the supernatural. Why, he showed me the tobacco pouch—you know he tells about that in his book——"

Peter nodded.

"Showed me, too, a handkerchief of his dead son's—— "

"That's not so remarkable."

"Yes, it is; 'cause it's one of a set that the chap took away with him, embroidered by his best girl, I believe."

Peter started. One of those handkerchiefs Carly gave him! Where in the world could that fool medium have got hold of that?

"Also a note from son, in his own handwriting," Douglas went on.

"Did you see it?"

"Yep. Commonplace looking note, advising his sister to drop acquaintance with Thorpe—he's the man they arrested in the Blair case."

"Where did the note come from?"

"Materialized—out of thin air."

"At a *seance?*"

"No; the brother kindly left it on sister's bureau, I believe."

Peter Crane was bewildered indeed. What sort of performances were going on, anyhow. And who was at the bottom of all this?

Clearly, he must look into things a little more before he did his final disappearance!

"Well, Mr. Douglas, you've helped me a whole lot. Now, as I say, I want mental impressions. Tell me everything you can think of about the atmosphere of the whole house, the—did you see Mrs. Crane?"

"No, only the old man. There seemed to be quite a lot of people about, coming and going. We had our interview in Mr. Crane's study, or library——"

"I know, the small room at the back of the house——"

"Been there?" Douglas looked up quickly.

"Read of it in the book," said Peter, quietly, annoyed at himself for the slip.

"Yes. Well, there's a table in the middle of the room, and in the drawer of that table Mr. Crane keeps all the things' materialized by the medium. I think he expects to get a big collection."

"Oh, Lord!" groaned Peter, "*what* a mess!"

"Yes, isn't it?" Douglas assumed that the whole subject of Spiritism was thus referred to.

"Suppose anything happened to shake Mr. Crane's faith?"

"I don't think anything *could* do that. He's absolutely gullible. He'd swallow anything. I say, how *do* you explain it? Why is it that big-brained, well-balanced men fall for this rot?"

"They can't be really well-balanced,—and then, too, it's largely the eagerness to believe, the desire for the comfort it brings them that makes them think they do believe. And a clever medium can do much."

"Sure. But those materializations! Where'd she get the goods?"

"Give it up. Tell me more about Mr. Crane."

So Douglas patiently recounted and repeated all the words of Peter's father and told of his appearance and manner, under the impression that he was helping an author with data for a psychological story.

Peter had found Douglas by merely making inquiry for a bright young reporter, and had made an agreement, satisfactory to both, for him to try to get the interview with Benjamin Crane, and they would both profit by it.

He was delighted that Crane had asked the young man to call again, and when they parted it was with the understanding that there should be another interview arranged.

Peter Boots had much food for thought.

He sat thinking for hours after the food had been given to him.

What was the explanation? What *could* be the explanation?

How could communications from a dead man be received when the man was not dead?

How he longed to go home, disclose himself, and run to earth that fearful fraud! How gladly he would do so, except that it would ruin his father's reputation. What would the public think of a man who had been so taken in by fraud, and had blazoned it to the world.

To be sure it was no reflection on Benjamin Crane's sincerity, yet he would be the butt of derision for the whole country, and his discredited head would be bowed for the rest of his life.

Peter couldn't bring himself to do that, especially now that he had discovered that his loss was not a source of hopeless grief to his parents.

"I'm not wanted in this world," he told himself, sadly, "I'm a superfluous man. I've got to dispose of myself somehow," and he gave a very realizing sigh.

And the thought of Carly,—that tried to obtrude itself, he put resolutely from him.

"She's probably forgotten me," he assured himself, "and anyway I must do the right thing by Mother and Dad first. If I decide that I can't demolish their air castle, so carefully built up, I must light out,—that's all."

Trying hard to be cheerful, but feeling very blue and desolate he ate a solitary dinner and went again to the theater to see "Labrador Luck."

Douglas' graphic description of his home and his father had given him a great longing to go there, to see the dear old place, the dear old man,—and his mother, and Julie.

He felt he *must* go. Then, he knew he couldn't go, without breaking his father's heart and life.

"I broke his heart when I *didn't* go home," he thought whimsically, "now, I mustn't break it again by going home!"

He sat through the moving picture performance again, and marveled anew at the beauty of the production. It was far above the rank and file of moving pictures, it was adjudged by all critics the very greatest production ever put upon the screen.

Shelby's name had become famous, his work was applauded everywhere, and Peter yearned to see him and renew their friendship.

But he knew he mustn't think of those things. First of all he had to decide whether or not he was to come back to life, and if not,—and he had a conviction that that would be his decision,—he must not dally with tempting thoughts and hopes of any sort.

But it was hard! Blair dead, Shelby famous, and he, Peter, unable to talk things over with any relative, chum or friend.

He must talk to somebody, and on his way out of the theater he spoke to the box office man.

"Wonderful show," he said, smiling at him. "Who's this Shelby?"

"He's the big push of to-day," was the enthusiastic reply. "He's a marvel of efficiency and generalship. And a big author, too."

"He wrote the play as well as produced it, I see."

"Yes. Oh, he can do anything."

"Married man?"

"No; but I've heard he's engaged to a girl,—a Miss Harper, I believe."

Peter choked. The last straw! But he might have known,—he, himself, supposed dead, Blair dead, what more natural than that Carly should turn to old Kit?

With a mere nod to the man who had unwittingly dealt him this final blow, Peter walked out into the night.

And he walked and walked. Up Broadway to the Circle, on up and into Riverside Drive, and along the Hudson as far as he could go.

Thinking deeply, planning desperately, only to be confronted with the awful picture of his father's consternation at the shattering of his beliefs and the collapse of his celebrity.

At times he would tell himself he was absurdly apprehensive, that any parents would rather have their lost son restored than to have the applause and notoriety of public fame. And, then, he would realize that while that might be generally true, yet this was a peculiar case. His father was a proud, sensitive nature. Perhaps—Peter shuddered,—perhaps he wouldn't love a son who by his return made him the most laughed at man in the whole world!

Peter longed to go to some one for advice. Shelby, now,—his big efficient mind would know at once what was best to do.

But he couldn't disclose himself to Kit and not to any one else. Kit couldn't keep that a secret, even if he wanted to do so.

And— Kit was engaged to Carly! He never wanted to see either of them again!

Poor, lonely, troubled Peter. Only one plain, sure truth abided. He *must* do his duty, and he felt pretty sure he knew what that duty was. It was to stay out of the life he had lost.

There was no other possible course.

He turned and retraced his steps southward, and finally went across town, drawn as by a magnet to his own home.

Home! What a mockery the word was!

It was two o'clock in the morning now; he had been walking or sitting on a Drive bench for hours.

He was not conscious of fatigue, he only wanted to see his old home and then go away forever. He didn't plan his future. He was sure he could make a living easily enough, he felt he could build up a new life for himself over a new name. But oh, how he longed for the old life!

He stood in front of the house and stared at it.

He walked round and round the block it was on, pausing each time he passed the front door, and walking on, if there chanced to be a passer-by.

At last, he concluded to give up the painful pleasure of gazing at the closed windows and go back to Brooklyn.

His gaze traveled over the windows at the various rooms,—how well he knew what they all were,—and at last he found himself looking at the front door. How often he had let himself in with his latchkey.

Involuntarily his hand went to his pocket, where that latchkey even now was,—and hardly knowing what he was doing, he had the key in his hand and was mounting the steps of his old home.

Still as one in a daze, and with no intention of making his presence known, but with an uncontrollable desire to see for the last time those dear rooms, he silently fitted the key into place.

Noiselessly he turned it and pushed the door open.

The house was still, there were no lights on, save a low glimmer in the front hall.

He remembered that had always been left on.

But the street lights faintly illumined the living-room, and he went in. With a wave of desperate homesickness he threw himself on the big davenport and buried his face into a pile of cushions.

He couldn't go away,—he *couldn't.*

But—he must!

And so, he forced himself to put aside his emotion, he bravely fought down his nostalgia, and promising himself one look into his father's study he vowed to go directly after.

He stepped into the little room where Douglas had been received. He couldn't resist the temptation to look about it, and, cautiously he snapped on the desk light.

There was the table with the drawer in it.

Carefully, Peter opened the drawer and saw for himself the tobacco pouch, the handkerchief, and the letter, signed "Peter."

He stared at it, amazed at the similarity to his own penmanship.

"I'd like to stay, if only to ferret out the mystery of this rascally fake!" he thought "But—oh, hang it! this rascally fake is the very breath of life to Dad and Mother. No, Peter Boots, it can't be done! You're out of it all and out of it all you must stay. Clear out of here now, before you get in any deeper."

He fingered the old tobacco pouch.

"Heavens and earth!" he exclaimed to himself, as a sudden thought struck him. "That's so!"

Again he took up the letter, looking closely at the formation of the words, studying the tenor of the message, and then, with a sigh, laid all back in the drawer and gently closed it.

"That way madness lies," he told himself, and turned to leave the room and the house.

As he reached for the light switch, a small hand laid on his own detained him.

Startled, he looked up and saw a witch-like, eerie face smiling at him.

"Must you go?" whispered a mocking voice, and Peter Boots, for once in his life was absolutely stricken dumb.

Who or what was this sprite, this Brownie? What was she doing in his father's house? Were materialized spirits really inhabiting the place?

"Hush!" Zizi warned him, "don't speak above a whisper. Are you a burglar?"

Peter shook his head, unable to repress a smile, and his smile made the same impression on Zizi that it had always made on everybody,—that of absolute pleasure.

"Who are you?" she asked, scarce breathing the words.

"John Harrison," he returned, still smiling. "I'll go now, please."

"Without further explanation?"

"Yes, please."

"All right, I'll let you out. I know all about you. You sent a chap here to interview Mr. Crane,—and you're getting follow-up literature."

"Right! Good night."

And with a swiftness and silence born of the dire necessity of the moment, Peter went to the front door, out of it and down the street in record time.

He turned the first corner, and walked rapidly many blocks, before turning to see if he were followed.

He was not, and he went on his way to Brooklyn, his life tragedy still ahead of him, but relieved by the touch of comedy added by that mysterious and wonderfully attractive girl.

CHAPTER 16: ZIZI'S OPPORTUNITY

The Blair case had come to a standstill. Although the police were still making investigations, they were fairly well satisfied that Thorpe was the guilty man and since he was jailed and awaiting trial, they rested on their laurels.

Pennington Wise was by no means sure of Thorpe's guilt, and Zizi was certain of his innocence, but though these two were working hard, as yet they had found no other definite suspect.

"But you must, Zizi," wailed Julie. "You know as well as I do that Mac never killed Gilbert. Now, find out who did!"

Wise confessed himself baffled, but asked for a little more time before admitting himself vanquished.

"You see, Ziz," he said to his astute young helper, "there are so many interesting side issues, that we get off the main track. I own up I'm quite as much absorbed in this Spiritism racket as I am in the murder case."

"That's the trouble, Penny," Zizi returned, gravely. "You're scattering your energies. And it won't do. You've got to concentrate on the Blair murder. And you've got to get at it from a different angle. Suppose you take a run out West and see that mother and sister. They may give you a line on things."

"I've been thinking I'd do that. There must be something in Blair's past that can be unearthed and may prove enlightening. I could do it in a week, and it might be time well spent."

"Of course it would. And, truly, there's no way to look, here. I've thought and thought but we've no hint or clew pointing to any one but Thorpe,—and, it wasn't Thorpe."

Then Zizi told him of the strange man she had seen in the Crane library the night before.

"And you let him get away! Why, Zizi?"

"He was no burglar. I saw that. There was no use in alarming the house. He was——"

"Well?"

"Oh, I knew at once who he was. He was the John Harrison who sent that Douglas person here to interview Mr. Crane."

"Well, is he to be allowed to walk in and out as he chooses! How did he get in?"

"I don't know, but I hope he'll come again. I like him. Why, Penny, he's a gentleman."

"But who is he? What's he up to?"

"He didn't confide in me, but I know. He's the medium's agent. He comes here and gets data and information and tells her and she works it off on the Cranes. I saw through that at once. He must have a key and he just walks in and helps himself, you see."

"Absurd!"

"Maybe; but that's what he does, all the same."

"And he told you his name!"

"Yes; but that's nothing. He'll have another name and another home before night. These mediums resort to the strangest tricks to get their stuff! Why, Penny, he was prowling in that drawer where the tobacco pouch is, and I think he meant to take it away so they could 'materialize' it over again. I'm going to watch for him nights. He'll come again."

But Zizi was mistaken. John Harrison did not come again, though the girl was alert to welcome him.

Pennington Wise went West, to see the relatives of Blair, for it had frequently been his experience that such inquiries into a man's early life brought about useful knowledge.

This left Zizi in a position of responsibility, to keep watch of developments and to learn what she could from them.

She was not so sure as Julie of Thorpe's innocence, but she meant to find another suspect if one could be found, and she redoubled her efforts.

Zizi had become a welcome guest in the Thorpe household, and they all admired and loved her. A most adaptable little piece, she fitted into the family as if she belonged there, and she and Julie were warm friends. She said nothing of the midnight intruder, being determined in her own mind, that he was an emissary from the medium, Madame Parlato, whom Zizi regarded as an absolute fake. To prove this was a desire of Zizi's mind as well as to solve the mystery of the Blair murder.

But her fondness for the Cranes was such, that she was not sure she should expose the medium's trickery, even if she discovered it herself. So she went on with her secret investigations, and at present they included an inquiry into the matter of that reporter's visit and John Harrison's appearance on the scene.

Zizi had, of course, read Benjamin Crane's book, and in it had seen the picture of Peter, but the portrait was so different in effect from the bearded man whom she saw but indistinctly by the dim light in the library that she never connected the two in her thoughts.

But she thoroughly believed that the man in the library had come there for the purpose of acquiring either information or materials for further manifestations of the medium. She was sure that the tobacco pouch and the handkerchief which had been "materialized" had been obtained in this way and, she argued, the best way to find out, was to remain silent as to John Harrison's call.

When told by Mr. Crane of the visit of Douglas, the reporter, Zizi had suspected something beneath the surface,—it did not seem plausible to her, that the case was just as it was stated.

And somehow, in the back of her astute little brain, she had a notion that the Blair murder and the supernatural manifestations were in some way connected, at least, indirectly.

So she was merely receptive, and put herself in the way of learning all she could of the medium's affairs without showing her own hand. She obtained a detailed account of the *seances* from the elder Cranes, and each time she became not only more convinced of the medium's fraud, but sure that the faker, more and more secure in her clients' credulity, was growing both daring and careless.

This, Zizi concluded, was her opportunity, and she hoped to profit by her knowledge of the visit of John Harrison.

*   *   *   *   *

And meantime, the so-called John Harrison, whom Zizi had sized up so mistakenly, was puzzling his head over the identity of the girl who had seen him.

He was not alarmed by fear of discovery, for he could change his name and address at will, but he was piqued by the saucy announcement that she knew all about him, and amazed at her knowledge that he had sent Douglas to see Benjamin Crane.

Moreover, the sight of that familiar old tobacco pouch of his own had stirred him, and some logical deductions that followed in its train caused him to reconsider his decision to disappear at once.

"But I got to have some money," he reasoned, "and I think I know how to get it!"

As a matter of fact, he did. He had in his mind a plot for a moving picture, which he had long cherished and thought over, but which he had never put on paper. The success of Shelby's great picture put it in his mind to try to sell his own. He was tempted to take it to the Shelby corporation but knowing it wiser, he went to a rival company.

As his plot was new, original and decidedly meritorious, he had no trouble in finding a market. He learned that he could sell merely his plot, that the "continuity" work would be done by their own people; and delighted to receive a most satisfactory lump sum, John Harrison gave his name as Louis Bartram, and removed to another hotel, where he registered under his new name.

For Peter Crane had resolved to do a little investigating on his own hook, and he realized that since the girl at his home knew his present cognomen it must be changed.

Louis Bartram, therefore, sent for Douglas, and took that mystified young man into his confidence to a degree.

"It's this way, Douglas," he said, "I give you my word I'm straight and all right, but I'm unraveling a mystery, and I'm incog for the present."

Now nobody could look into Peter Crane's blue eyes and doubt his veracity, and Douglas believed exactly what was told him.

"Can I help?" he said, simply, and Louis Bartram told him he could.

Wherefore, Bartram expeditiously acquired such information as he needed, and the first item was the name and address of the medium who was responsible for the *seances* detailed in Benjamin Crane's famous book.

And then to the house of Madame Parlato, Louis Bartram went, having made an appointment through the useful Douglas.

The madame's quick glance of inquiry was satisfied and her ever-ready suspicions lulled by her first glance into Peter's eyes. It was impossible to distrust that frank gaze, and though Peter was an unbeliever in her and all her works, yet his cause was honest and sincere and he met her on her own ground.

"You want a *seance*?" the occult lady inquired.

"No, Madame Parlato," Peter returned, quietly, "I want to bribe you to undertake a commission for me."

"Wh—what!" she cried, turning white and quite losing her poise at his astonishing remark.

"Now, let's cut out all that," Peter went on, practically, "let's assume that we've thrashed it all out, and agreed that you're one of the cleverest of your sort and can fool the gullible ones very neatly. But, let's also assume that when one who knows comes along that you will meet him halfway, and at least, listen to his proposition."

"But, this,—this is outrageous——"

"Not at all. You see, I know of the faking you have done,—and are doing,—in the Crane matter."

"Oh,—ah——" Madame cautiously awaited further speech from her attractive but unusual caller.

"Yes,—and," here Peter made a bold stroke, "I know who is giving you things to 'materialize,' and why, and I want to know how much you are being paid, in order that I may offer you more to follow my directions."

"I do not acknowledge that you are right——" she began, but Peter interrupted:

"You needn't; your expression, your countenance tells me all I want of acknowledgment. Now, listen to reason. I only want one *seance*, conducted according to my orders, and I'll pay you what you demand. Your other patron needn't know anything about my hand in the matter."

"I refuse your requests, sir. I resent your accusations, and unless you leave here at once, I shall call——"

"Oh, no, you won't call the police, or any one else. You would greatly object to an investigation of your place here, and you and I know why. You'll do much better, madame, to listen to my proposition, and accept it. You see,— I *know*!"

The mysterious tone Peter used seemed to carry conviction, and with a little shudder, Madame Parlato gave in.

"What do you want?" she asked, tremulously; "what do you intend to do?"

"I intend to do a great many things," Peter replied, gravely, "but I want very little. Only that you shall conduct a *seance*, at the time I set and entirely in accordance with my orders."

"And if I refuse?"

"Then I shall feel it my duty to expose you as a fraud and a charlatan."

The woman winced at these words, but meeting Peter's steely gaze and realizing his power over her, she said:

"First, tell me who you are."

"I am Louis Bartram," he said, "you know that already. For the rest, I am an investigator of psychic conditions and a student of the occult, along certain definite lines. You will find it to your best advantage, Madame, to be perfectly frank and truthful with me. Any other course you will find most disastrous."

"Are you—are you of the——"

"Of the police? No, this is not an official investigation. And, moreover, it all depends on yourself whether the results of our work together are ever made public or not. Now, answer my questions. How did you come to give these *seances* to the Cranes?"

"Mr. Crane came and asked me to."

"Where had he heard of you?"

"I was recommended to him by some friends of his."

"Did you ever know his son, Peter?"

"No; I never heard of him until Mr. Crane came here."

"And then you immediately got into spiritual communication with the dead man?"

"Yes; that is my business."

She spoke a little defiantly, and Peter smiled. "I know. I accept that. Now, I'm a friend of the Cranes, because of having read that book. A man who is so absolutely positive of his beliefs is too good and dear a man to be disturbed in his enjoyment of them."

"Oh, Mr. Bartram, I'm glad you see it that way, too! Truly, I've come to love the Cranes, and if—if I help along a little, it is largely for the comfort and happiness it gives them."

"I know,— I see; and I realize what an awful thing it would be if the world were to learn that all the matter in his book is really false——"

"Oh, it would kill him! If you knew Mr. Crane, if you knew how his very life is bound up in this matter, you would be even more assured what a disaster it would be to have him in any way discredited!"

Peter's heart fell at this, for he had a half hope that he could yet bring himself to demolish his father's air castle.

"Well, then," he said, slowly, "I'll not discredit him, nor you, for, of course, one involves the other. But this, on condition that you obey my commands implicitly in this matter of a *seance*. If you fail me in one particular, if you disobey one tiny detail, or, if you so much as hint a word to your—your other employer,—I mean the one who has bribed you to certain frauds,—then, I shall show you up, even if it does distress Mr. and Mrs. Crane."

Madame Parlato thought in silence for a moment. Then she said, astutely, "I don't know who you are, Mr. Bartram, but I am quite certain you are something more than you wish to tell. I mean a bigger factor in the Crane affair than you admit. I ask no questions, I agree to your terms, and I will do exactly as you direct, relying on your promise that if I do so, you will not tell of any—any insincerity you may notice."

"Wait a moment,—that promise may lead to complications. If the result of my proposed procedure is to reveal your—er,—insincerity—I cannot be responsible for the consequences. Those you will have to bear. But I will admit that my interests are those of Benjamin Crane, and I shall do all in my power to preserve his secrets and, thereby, yours."

"I think, then, you may go ahead and tell me your plans that you wish me to carry out."

"I've revised them,'" Peter said, thoughtfully, "they may, as I now see it, call for more than one *seance*. But here's for a starter. When do you expect Mr. Crane again?"

"To-morrow."

"All right. Merely give him a further materialization. And let the object be this,"—he laid a small paper parcel before her, which he had taken from his pocket,—"yes,— and this," and he produced a second parcel.

She opened the papers, and found the first to be a handkerchief, the duplicate of the one already "materialized" and bearing the monogram Carly had so painstakingly embroidered.

The other parcel contained a silver quarter of a dollar, one side of which had been smoothed off and engraved with the entwined letters P. C.

"These belonged to the son?" Madame exclaimed, excitedly. "Where did you get them?"

"From the son," replied Louis Bartram; "but remember you are under oath of secrecy. You are merely to produce these things as materializations at your next session with Mr. Crane, and also,—I want to be present,—unseen. Can it be managed?"

"Of course, that's easy enough."

Further arrangements were made, terms were agreed on, and Louis Bartram went away from the house of the medium in New York and returned to his hotel in Brooklyn.

And as he came down the steps of the Parlato residence, a small, dark girl, who was walking by, quickly scuttled around a corner, and out of his line of vision.

"I knew it!" Zizi said to herself, exultantly, "he's in cahoots with the spook woman! He's been there to give her things to materialize and soon I'll hear of them! He came to the house and stole something which she will use to fool poor old Mr. Crane. You'll see!"

Zizi talked enthusiastically to herself, resolving to learn more of this attractive young man's identity.

"Clever, wasn't he?" she asked of herself, "to send that reporter around first,—probably he stole a key to the house,—oh, it's a whole big organization, I suppose, and they cover their tracks so completely they're not even suspected."

Acting on an impulse, she turned and went back to the house of the medium. By strategy, she succeeded in getting an interview, although she had no appointment.

"I have come to warn you," she said, without preamble, looking into the woman's eyes, "I am a detective, and I am onto your game. I know that man who just left here, he is your tool, your accomplice. Also, I know that he stole some things from the Crane house that you intend to use in your so-called materializations. Now, I warn you that if you do that, I shall see to it that your deceit is shown up, your fraud exposed!"

"My Lord," cried the puzzled Madame, "who are you? Why do you think that man is my accomplice? It is not so! I never laid eyes on him until this morning!"

"That is not true," Zizi said, sure of her ground, and wondering why the medium looked so unfeignedly puzzled. "He works for you——"

"He does not! He is a client. Now you leave, or I'll have you put out."

"I am going to leave," and Zizi rose, "but you remember what I said. If you show up any more materialized belongings of Mr. Crane's dead son, I'll have you exposed and arrested!"

It is doubtful which of the two was more perplexed by this conversation.

Zizi, with her quick reading of human nature, saw that Madame Parlato was truly surprised at the girl's accusation of an accomplice, therefore, she decided, he could not be an accomplice, after all. And if not, what was he, and what was he doing at the medium's house?

That he was a client, she did not believe, for had she not seen him, rummaging in the Crane library and in that table drawer? It was all most mysterious and Zizi determined to stick to this new mystery in hopes it would shed some light on the old ones.

Meanwhile Madame Parlato was absolutely bewildered. Who was this strange girl who had come flying in with an incredible tale about the new client being an accomplice of her own?

Nor did that question trouble her so much as the consideration of what she should do next? She had arranged to have Mr. Crane at a *seance* the next evening, and to have Mr. Louis Bartram concealed in an adjoining room, where he could see and hear without being discovered.

Now, if she failed to use the objects he had directed her to use she feared his ire and vengeance, while if she did use them, this awful child, who called herself a detective, threatened exposure!

To be sure, she told herself, that little scrap of humanity couldn't be a detective, the thought was impossible. Yet the child's words and tones had carried conviction. Indeed, she was no child, though small enough to be one. She was either a detective, the Madame finally decided, or, she was a fake medium herself, and had some unknown ax to grind.

In any case, the way of the transgressor was hard, and the occult lady thought a long time before she came to a decision.

But the conclusion she reached was to obey the orders of Louis Bartram. He was a far more formidable antagonist, there must be more real danger in disobeying him than that chit of a girl.

So Madame laid her plans, prepared her properties, and, with fear in her heart, arranged for the forthcoming *seance*.

And Zizi, worried and uncertain, in Wise's absence, as to just what she should do, laid her plans to be present also at Benjamin Crane's next session with the medium.

And Peter Boots, communing with himself, and rapidly getting more and more excited at his discoveries and the developments of his theories, impatiently awaited the hour when he should see his father and perhaps his mother.

CHAPTER 17: THE HEART HELPER

Never during her association with Wise, had Zizi wanted him so much as she did at present. The situation, she felt, was too big for her to handle, and the contradictory conclusions forced upon her bewildered her.

Public interest in the Blair murder had waned, or at least it was waiting for the trial of McClellan Thorpe, and while the police were ready to listen to any new evidence or theories, none seemed to be forthcoming.

Julie was in despair, feeling that the great Pennington Wise was making no headway in his endeavors to free Thorpe, and Benjamin Crane too was beginning to doubt Wise's ability.

Zizi, therefore, felt the brunt of upholding her colleague's reputation for cleverness and success, and now that things were getting so complicated, and Penny Wise so far away, the girl felt her responsibility almost greater than she could bear.

But, she concluded, after deep thought, the first and most important thing to be done was to locate that John Harrison.

From Benjamin Crane she obtained the address of young Douglas, the reporter, and went to see him.

Douglas was greatly pleased with the appearance and manner of his visitor, for Zizi was at her sparkling best, and that was very good indeed.

"You see, Mr. Douglas," she confided with a captivating smile, "I'm a Heart Helper."

"A what?"

"Yes. I help people's hearts,—people who are sad or in trouble. Now, I'm working in the interests of a dear friend, a lovely girl, whose sweetheart is being most unjustly treated, and only I can set things straight. Think of that!"

The great dark eyes flashed an appealing glance at him, and Zizi's red mouth took a sorrowful droop at the corners.

Instinctively he yearned to bring back the smile and he said, promptly, "Can I help you? Is that why you come to me?"

"Exactly," and Zizi beamed at him, quite completing his undoing.

"And what I want," she went on quickly, lest she lose her suddenly-acquired power over him, "is only the address of Mr. John Harrison."

Douglas's face fell, and he plainly showed his embarrassment and chagrin.

"That I can't tell you," he began,—but paused at the look of despair that came to Zizi's expressive face.

"Oh, please," she begged. "It's so necessary,—so important. I won't make any wrong use of the information. Please tell me."

"But I can't, Miss Zizi. You see, Mr.—Harrison isn't where he was. He—he isn't anywhere."

Clearly, Douglas thought, he was making a mess of things. But what could he say?

"Are you making game of me?" Zizi's tone was wistful, and with her head cocked to one side like an alert bird, she waited breathlessly for his answer.

"No, not a bit of it!"

"But—you say—he isn't anywhere! What do you mean?"

Still under the spell of her smile, her fascinating manner, and her sweet, piquant little face, Douglas hesitated,—and was lost.

"Well, you see, he,—he was somebody else. I mean he isn't,—that is, he isn't himself."

"Are you sure you are?" Zizi laughed outright, so infectiously, that Douglas joined in.

"No, I'm not!" he admitted. "Now, if you're not, either, we're all in the same boat."

But Zizi was not to be put off with foolery.

"Mr. Douglas," she said, seriously, "truly, I'm on an important errand, and one involving grave consequences. You can help greatly by giving me that man's address, and help not only the girl of whom I spoke, but help the cause of right and justice, even, perhaps, in a matter of life and death. Don't refuse——"

"But if I don't refuse, I must at least inquire. And, suppose I tell you that Mr. Harrison does not want his address known?"

"I assumed that. But, suppose I tell you that it may help to clear up one of the greatest mysteries of the day if you will just give me a hint where I can find that man. And, even though he has forbidden you to tell, I think I can assure you that he won't mind my knowing the secret, and if he does mind I'll persuade him to exonerate you."

Zizi had meant to take quite a different tack,—use hints of legal authority or suggest his duty to humanity, but intuition told her that this man was best persuaded by coaxing,—and Zizi could coax!

She succeeded only partly. After she convinced Douglas of the wisdom of such a course he told her that John Harrison had been at the Hotel Consul in Brooklyn, but had left there, and had left no further address.

Moreover, he declared he had no knowledge whatever of the whereabouts of John Harrison at the present time.

"No!" and Zizi flashed a quizzical smile, "because he has changed his name! I know that from your emphatic declaration! But I'll find him. Good-by."

Zizi betook herself forthwith to the Hotel Consul.

A polite clerk informed her that Mr. Harrison had checked out, leaving no address.

Determinedly she interviewed the cab drivers ranked in front of the hotel, and by a lucky chance found the one who had driven Mr. Harrison away. A proper bribe brought the knowledge that he had been driven to the Wilfer, a much smaller hotel nearby.

To the Hotel Wilfer Zizi went, and learned there was no John Harrison there, but a very few inquiries proved to her astute intellect that the Louis Bartram, who was the only guest registered at that time on that afternoon, was in all probability the man she sought. At any rate there was no harm in trying.

She asked for an interview, and was connected with Mr. Bartram's rooms by telephone.

"I want to see you again," she said, in response to his Hello,—"Let me come up, Mr. Midnight Visitor, please."

Partly the pleading voice, partly the fact that Peter was eager for new developments in his devious course, and partly a sudden recollection of the girl he had seen in his father's library, brought about a cordial invitation to "come along."

And Zizi exultantly went, hoping against hope that she was on her way to learn something of real importance.

For so many hopeful openings had proved blind alleys, so many bright prospects of success had dimmed on nearer view, that Zizi had begun to lose heart, and this seemed to her perhaps a last chance.

Peter received her in his sitting room, and as the big dark eyes looked deep into the chicory blue ones, and both smiled, it was impossible to be formal.

"Why are you a burglar, Mr. Bartram," Zizi said, as she seated herself sociably in the depths of a big armchair. "You don't look the part a bit."

"What is *your* calling?" he countered; "for unless it is that of a witch or Brownie, I'm sure *you* don't look it."

"I am all of those things," she announced, calmly, crossing her dainty feet and gazing guilelessly at him. "I'm a witch, a Brownie, a sprite, an elf, a kobold, a pixie——"

"That's enough. They're all tarred with the same brush. And why am I favored with this angel visit?"

"So you may answer my question, which you so rudely ignored. Why are you a burglar?"

"But I'm not. Can your ingenuity suggest no explanation of a man's presence in another man's house at midnight save a burglarious motive? I took no jewels nor plate away with me."

"So you didn't. But, I admit motives seem scarce. You were not intending a social call, were you? You didn't come to read the meter or repair the plumbing? You were not seeking a lodging for the night?"

"None of those, Miss Brownie. But, why am I obliged to tell?"

"Because I ask it," and Zizi's pretty powers of coaxing were put to the utmost test.

"I admit that constitutes an obligation, but, I am not going to meet it," and the big man settled back comfortably in his chair and smiled benignly but a trifle exasperatingly.

"Then,—" and the little brown face became serious, the merry light went out of the dark eyes, and Zizi said, coldly, "Then I will tell you. You are a burglar,—you did take valuables from Mr. Crane's house,—at least they were valuable to you, though perhaps of small intrinsic worth."

"Whatever *do* you mean?"

"I mean that you are the accomplice of that woman who calls herself a medium,—that woman who is a fraud, a fake, a miserable charlatan! You came to the house to get some more belongings of Mr. Crane's dead son's,—in order to take them to the Parlato woman and let her trade further on an old man's credulity! That's what you were there for!"

Zizi's nerves were at high tension. She thoroughly believed every word she said, and she felt that perhaps the best way to make this man own up was to put the case thus straightforwardly.

Peter Boots looked at her, his expression changing from amazement to amusement and then to sympathy.

"No," he said gently, "I didn't do that. I swear I didn't."

"Then why were you there?"

Uncertain what to say, Peter just sat and looked at her.

And somehow,—by some subtle intelligence or telepathic flash—all of a sudden,—Zizi knew!

"Oh," she breathed, her eyes like stars, "oh,—you're Peter Boots!"

Slowly, Peter nodded his head.

"Yes," he said, "I am. Now, what are we going to do about it?"

"Do about it? Why, everything! Oh,—wait a minute,— let me take it in,—let me think what it will mean——"

"To father? Yes, I know."

These two, so lately strangers, were immediately at one. Zizi, with her instantaneous understanding and quick appreciation saw the whole situation at once, and realized fully its tragedy.

"It can't be, you know," she cried out; "it mustn't be! Think of the——"

"I know," returned Peter, "I've thought."

Instead of being appalled at the knowledge that his secret was out, Peter felt a positive relief, a sudden let-down of his strained nerves, and a queer sensation of confidence in this strange girl's powers to set things right.

Peter's intuitions were quick and true; Zizi was not only charming, but gave an effect of capability and efficiency that were as balm and comfort to poor, harassed Peter.

He was willing to nail his colors to her mast; to give his affairs and perplexities into her hands; to abide by her decisions.

And Zizi accepted the tremendous responsibility gravely.

"But it is all too wonderful," she said. "What happened? Where have you been?"

"Two broken legs,—compound fractures,—frozen feet,—gangrene—ugh!—fierce—cut it out!"

"The gangrene!" cried Zizi, horrified.

"Yes, but I didn't mean that. I meant can the description of my sufferings! They'd put the early Christian martyrs to the blush. They would indeed! But let's take up the tale from the present moment."

"Oh, wait a minute,—do! Who rescued you? Why haven't you——"

"Lumbermen,—camp, miles from any sort of a lemon. Couldn't get into communication. Fiercest winter ever known,—everything cut off from everything else. Came home the minute I could,—and,—oh, thunder! how I want to know things! Tell me heaps, do! And who are you, anyway?"

"Heavens, what a tale! Yes, I'll tell you everything, but what shall I fly at first? And—oh, I can't stand the responsibility of your secret! I can't! Why are you keeping it secret? On account of your father?"

"Yes, that's the sole reason. How can I come forward,—the son who is supposed dead,—who is supposed to come back as a spook,—the son who has had a book written about him——"

"Oh, what a situation! And your father so wrapped up in the whole business,—so positive in his beliefs——"

"And that rascally medium!"

"And those wicked materializations!"

"And the fool Ouija Board!"

"And that letter from you to Julie—oh, I say!"

"And *I* say! But, tell me, what can I do? Do you see it as I do? That I must go away again, disappear forever,—or——"

"Or break your father's heart,— I mean,—oh, I don't know what I mean! Mr. Peter, I think I'll lose my mind!"

"I've almost lost mine, puzzling over the thing. But I've put the kibosh on that Parlato!"

"Oh, that's why you were there! I got things all wrong, didn't I? And you came to your own home——"

"Only because of a terrible attack of homesickness. You see, I still have my latch key, and if you hadn't seen me, I should have merely had a good look around, and then silently steal away, without, however, stealing anything else!"

Zizi smiled at her accusation of his burglarious intent, and then sat musing.

"I can't grapple with it," she said, at last. "It's too big. I shall telegraph for Mr. Wise. He must come back at once and help us."

"Now, look here, Miss Zizi, I'm not lying down on this job myself. I'm not asking you to carry my burdens or fight my battles. I am very much able to hoe my own row,—only I fear it's going to be a hard one. I'm going to depend on you for help, if I may, but I'll take the helm; Peter Boots leads, he doesn't follow."

Zizi gazed at him, her eyes moist with emotional admiration. This man, this splendid, fine man,—to efface himself to save his father's reputation,—it was too bad! She couldn't stand it.

"Now, wait," she began; "wouldn't your father,—your mother,—rather have you back with them in the flesh,— than to have their pride spared?"

"Answer that yourself," he returned. "I admit that if that question were put to them, they would doubtless say yes. But that's not the thing. The point is, they're reconciled to my loss, happy in the experiences they're having,—delusions though they are,—and contented, even exultant, in things as they are. Why disturb that happiness, for my selfish reasons? Why not leave them to their Fools' Paradise,—for that's what it is,—and not take the chance of what might easily be a distressing disillusion?"

"It would indeed be that," Zizi spoke gravely; "I know it would. But what will you do?"

"Go 'way off somewhere,—start fresh,—make a new name and fame for myself and forget——"

"Sacrifice your own identity to your father's reputation?"

"Exactly that,—and, simply, it is my duty."

"And Carlotta Harper?"

Peter jumped.

"Tell me about Carly," he said, speaking thickly. "Is she engaged to Shelby?"

"No, she isn't!"

"I heard she was."

"Probably he hinted it, and the report started. He's eternally after her, but, to my certain knowledge she hasn't yet said yes."

"Oh, my God! Dear little Carly! What can I do?"

"She would go with you,—into a new life——"

"No; don't be absurd! This secret must be kept inviolably. Nor could I marry her under an assumed name, even if she were willing. Also, she may have forgotten me."

"No, she has not. Oh, Mr. Peter, you must come home."

"I can't. But tell me more,—tell me of mother, of Julie,—why, I sent a reporter to the house just to get a line on home life,—on present conditions,—oh, little girl, you don't know what I suffered; it's all so foolish,—so absurd,—the spook stuff, I mean,—yet, as I've learned, it's the very breath of life to my Dad."

"It is; but, look at the thing from another angle. Couldn't you help unravel the Blair mystery. Here's Mr. Thorpe held for a crime I don't think he committed; here's Julie crying her eyes out because of it——"

"Julie! She and Thorpe!"

"Yes, didn't you know that?"

"No; are they engaged?"

"In a way. If Thorpe should be freed Mr. Crane will give his consent. If Thorpe is convicted——"

"He shan't be convicted! He never killed Blair! I'll find out who killed Blair, and then I'll go away after that. I'll help Julie,—why, Thorpe wouldn't kill Gilbert, why should he?"

"You've read the case?"

"Yes, and thought how little evidence there was against Thorpe. But, I'm ashamed to say, my own affairs rather blotted the matter out. But if Julie's concerned, that's another matter. I'll free Thorpe,—and I can do it, too!"

"Then it's most certainly your duty, for many reasons. Look here, Mr. Peter, don't let your ideas of duty get over-sentimental regarding your father."

"Oh, I don't!" Peter waxed impatient. "But I've mulled over the thing to the very end, and I know, I *know* father would be happier left to his delusions. Yes, and mother, too. You see, I've read the book, and knowing Dad as I do, I read between the lines, and I see how it would be like stabbing his heart and draining his life blood to stultify that book. No, Zizi, don't tempt me,—indeed, you can't."

"Well, then, come back to the murder case. Have you any suspect other than Thorpe?"

"Why, sometimes, I think I have. But it's a serious thing to accuse, without evidence. Now, I think I can get evidence, but mainly from Madame Parlato. You see, she has been bribed by a powerful influence,—she is absolutely under orders from some one, and it is because of that she is so frightened for fear of exposure. I think in the ordinary *seance* with my father, where my spirit— ugh!—appears and talks guff and rubbish, the medium is more fool than knave. But when the spirit gives information concerning the murderer,—and wrong information,—it's criminal work itself, and ought to be shown up."

"Showing up the medium would expose the falsity of your father's book, even without your reappearance."

"I've thought of that, but there's duty there, too. If I can free Mac Thorpe from unjust accusations, and incidentally, I'm thinking of Julie,—it's in all ways my duty to do so,—even if——"

"Even if it makes your father a butt for ridicule."

"Yes, even that. All things are matters of comparison. Thorpe's life, or even Thorpe's name mustn't be sacrificed to father's feelings. I may sacrifice my own future, even my own life if I choose, but not that of another."

"Are you sure Mr. Thorpe is innocent?"

"As sure as shooting! But you must tell me all the details of your investigations. I've studied the newspaper reports, but I want your accounts, too. When can you get Wise back here? Send for him at once, will you? He can't get anything on Blair out there. Blair's life was blameless. I know it as I know my own. Why, Zizi, you don't realize,— I've lived with my family and my friends for a whole long lot of years. I'm no newcomer, except regarding the last six months. You can't tell me of Blair's character, or Thorpe's either. Now, what I want to puzzle out is whether I can do my part in producing the real murderer, without revealing my presence here and without even showing my hand in the matter."

"You might appear as your own spook."

"I've thought of that, and it offers wide possibilities. But it isn't fair to mother and Dad. Let the medium fool them, if she will, it's not for their own son to fool them, too! No, I can't do that."

"You might appear to the—the criminal."

"And give him the scare of his life! Yes, I might do that. But I'm not yet sure he is the criminal,—I'm basing my suspicion on generalities, not any specific evidence."

"Tell me his name."

"Not yet. Let's plan a little first. You see, I've arranged a fake *seance* with Madame Parlato. If I rearrange it a bit, it may serve our purpose. I'll postpone it until Mr. Wise can get back, and then we'll see what we shall see!"

CHAPTER 18: THE CONFESSION

Peter Boots arranged and rearranged his plans for the *seance* many times.

Though still living under the name of Louis Bartram, he had cast aside fear of having his real identity discovered, pretty sure, now, that it must come sooner or later.

His present concern was with the discovery of Blair's murderer, and thereby the freeing of his sister's fiance. These accomplished he would consider the case of his own restored identity, if it were not by that time a foregone conclusion.

Pennington Wise came back from the West, and was let into the secret.

His amazement was beyond all bounds when Zizi took him over to the Brooklyn hotel and he met Peter Crane.

"This thing has never been equaled in my experience," he declared. "And no one but Zizi could have found you out, unless you chose to make yourself known. Now, we must move warily,—your quarry may get away."

"You know whom I suspect?" asked Peter in astonishment.

"Of course I do, and I've had the same suspect from the beginning. But I couldn't get a shred of evidence,—haven't any yet,— I say, Mr. Crane, suppose you confide in me fully. You'll have no cause to regret it."

So Peter Boots and Pennington Wise and Zizi had a long confab, in which all cards were laid on the table, and all details of the plan settled.

Wise agreed that it would be a fearful blow to Benjamin Crane's pride, but he held that the author of the book about Peter would receive no blame and the fame of the affair would be world-wide, which would make up for the blow to the author's vanity.

Peter was not convinced of this, but agreed to go ahead as Wise suggested. Indeed, he had no choice, for it now rested on his statements whether an innocent man was tried for crime or not.

The medium was completely suborned. She was instructed that if she obeyed orders implicitly and succeeded in fulfilling the desires of her new employers, she would be paid a large sum of money, and enabled to leave the country secretly and safety.

For, after all, she was doing no more than the great army of "mediums" all over the world, and if she achieved good at last, they wished no harm to come to her.

"Moreover," as Peter said, "she was a great comfort to my parents in my absence, and when they know of my presence, they'll have no further use for Madame!"

The *seance* was staged in the Crane home.

It was a simple matter for Madame Parlato to persuade Benjamin Crane to allow her to hold a session there, promising him a probable materialization of his son, if allowed to attempt it in the scenes familiar to Peter Boots.

It was pathetic to see the hope and joy on the faces of Peter's father and mother as they were offered this experience. Gladly they accepted the proposition, and when the medium further advised them to invite a few friends, they willingly did so.

It was not announced that materialization was expected,—Madame Parlato preferred it should not be, she said; so the friends were merely asked to a *seance*.

After all, Zizi, who had charge of the invitations informed them, interest must be falling off, for no one was coming except Miss Harper, who would also bring Mr. Shelby.

However, with the Crane household, that made quite a group, and as Detective Weston had heard about it, and asked to be present he also had a seat, in the rear of the room.

There was no air of secrecy, the waiting audience were receptive, hopeful or skeptical as their natures prompted.

Shelby and Carlotta whispered to each other that they were glad to see a specimen of the genius that had hoaxed so able a mind as Benjamin Crane's. Julie was out of sorts and sad, for she disliked the whole subject, and pitied her father and mother for their absorption in it.

At last Madame Parlato appeared.

She was an impressive looking woman, tall, slender, and with the traditional long green eyes and red hair. Her face was very white, but she was calm and well-poised, and seemed to feel a great sense of responsibility.

She had not been informed of Peter's identity, but she knew him to be acquainted with the man whom she still considered dead, and she knew that Mr. Bartram was to impersonate Peter Crane.

She asked the eight people present to sit in a circle and join hands, allowing herself to make one of them.

Weston flatly refused to do this, saying he preferred to sit alone at the back of the room. He did so, and took his place near the door of the small library of Mr. Crane's, the session being held in the large living room.

The medium requested that the lights be shut entirely off, saying that sufficient illumination would come in from the street to prevent total darkness.

This proved to be true, and the dim light was just enough for them to distinguish one another's forms but not faces.

"Poppycock," whispered Shelby to Carlotta, as he held her hand.

Zizi, who sat on Shelby's other side, heard it and answered, "Absolutely."

Then the usual things happened. The medium went into a trance state, and the regular proceedings took place.

She gave messages to Mr. Crane, purporting to be from his dead son. She gave messages to Julie and to Peter's mother, all vapid and meaningless and mentally scoffed at by all present, except the two elderly listeners.

At last the medium said, "I am weary,—weary,—I would sleep. The spirit of Peter Crane himself would speak to you."

"Will you?" eagerly asked Benjamin Crane, "will you speak yourself, Peter?"

"Yes, father," came a reply, and everybody started.

Surely that was Peter's own voice! Not loud, almost a whisper, but with the unmistakable cadence and tone of Peter, himself.

"That's Peter!" cried Julie, excitedly, "oh, father, is it?"

"Hush, dear," her father said, himself greatly agitated. "One must be very calm and quiet on these occasions. Peter Boots, will you talk with us?"

"Gladly, Dad," came the voice again,—seeming to emanate from behind Detective Western's chair,—as indeed it did.

"Then tell us of yourself, my boy."

Mrs. Crane said no word, but sat, her hand in that of her husband, full of faith in the genuineness of it all, and ready to listen and believe.

"I am very happy here, father," Peter's voice declared,—and Zizi bit her lip to keep from smiling at the hackneyed phrase uttered by mortal tongue!

"You sound so real, Peter," Julie said, bluntly. "Is it always like this?"

For Julie had never attended a *seance* before.

"No, sister," the voice said, speaking more clearly with every word; "this is an unusual occasion. Perhaps,— perhaps the medium can bring about materialization to-night."

"Oh, don't," Julie cried out, "I'm scared!"

"Don't be frightened, Julie," Peter said, his voice faint again, "I won't hurt you."

The well-remembered gentleness reassured Julie, and she held tight to her parents' hands and listened.

"I have a message for each of you," the voice went on; "or you may each ask me a question, as you prefer."

"I'll ask," Julie exclaimed; "Peter, dear Peter Boots, tell me that Mac never killed Gilbert. I know it, yet I want you to say so. They told me you didn't know, and that you were misinformed and all that. You do know, don't you, Peter?"

"Yes, Julie, I know. And Mac didn't kill Gilbert at all. But I know who did. Shall I tell?"

"Yes," cried out several in chorus.

And then, from out the dark shadows behind Weston's chair, there slowly appeared a dark, cloaked form. A black-draped, hooded figure, that moved slowly toward them. A tall, big figure that seemed to loom out of the darkness, and then the hood fell back a little, a white ghostly face appeared dimly and a slowly raised hand pointed to Kit Shelby.

"Thou art the man!" came in low, accusing tones, and they were unmistakably Peter's.

Julie shrieked, and the accused man gave a strange, guttural sound, expressive of abject fear, and as the tall figure drew nearer, he rose to flee from its avenging shape.

Shelby didn't go far, for his progress was stopped by the burly form of Detective Weston, who advised him to sit down.

"Confess!" went on the figure that seemed to be Peter, and with wild eyes, fairly starting from their sockets at the sight, Shelby cried out, "I did, oh, Peter, I did!" and then he fell in a convulsion of fright and terror.

And then, Peter Boots himself switched on the lights, threw off his long cloak, and turned to take his mother in his arms.

"My boy, my boy!" she said, knowing intuitively and instantaneously that it was her son, alive and found.

Benjamin Crane was a picture of utter perplexity. Unable to accept the obvious, he tried for a moment to believe in a marvelous "materialization," but Peter came to him, smiling and holding out an eager hand.

"Welcome me home, Dad," he said, a quiver in his strong voice. "I know what a shock it is, but brace up and meet it,— I'm here, and very much alive. In fact, I never have been dead at all."

"Peter,—Peter," his father muttered, and fearing ill effects, Zizi came quickly to his side.

"Yes, Mr. Crane," she said in her brisk little way. "Peter Boots, home again. Never mind the spook stuff now. Cut it out,—forget it,—let him tell us of his adventures."

And now Carly came toward Peter.

One glance passed between them, and she was in his arms, a smiling, sweet Carly, who kissed him right before everybody, and said triumphantly, "I knew you'd come back!"

"Of course," said Peter, happily holding her to him. "I had to, the gypsies prophesied it, you know. They didn't mean come back as a silly old spirit, they meant come back in the flesh, and here I am. Kit, old man, I'm sorry."

And there was infinite sorrow and pity in the face that Peter turned on Shelby, who was still trembling and mouthing in a vain effort to speak.

"Get his confession," said Wise, lest when the shock wore off Shelby might dare deny it all.

But he couldn't speak, and out of very pity, Peter said, "I'll tell the details, and Shelby can nod assent."

"Go ahead," said Weston, his eye on his prisoner.

"I'll not tell of my experiences now, only to say there is no blame to be attached to Shelby or to Blair or to the guide for my accident. I fell in the snow, and somehow so managed to double my half-frozen legs under me that the silly things both broke. I floundered in the drifts but couldn't get up, nor could I make the boys hear my shouts, for the wind was against me. Well, I was picked up—after many hours—by some lumbermen and my tale of woe thereafter would fill a set of books. But never mind that now, I got home just as soon as I possibly could, having been absolutely unable to get a letter here any sooner than I could come myself. I came back to find that Dad, supposing me dead, had written a book,—oh, my eye! Dad, how you did butter me! Well, then I was up a stump to know whether to make my joyous presence known and spill the beans entirely or whether to sneak off, disappear forever and leave Dad to his laurel and bay."

"Peter! how could you dream of such a thing!" Benjamin Crane was himself now. "I'd a million times rather have you back than to have written all the books in the world!"

"But, father, think what people will say! I understand your book is read and discussed from pole to pole——"

"And it may be hooted at from pole to pole for all I care! Oh, Peter! Peter Boots! Good old chap!"

Peter's blue eyes beamed. The thing that had worried him most had turned out all right. Moreover, Carly seemed still kindly disposed toward him.

Remained only the dreadful business of Shelby and that must be put through.

"Then," Peter resumed, "I came home, and found old Gilbert Blair was dead. Murdered. And Mac Thorpe arrested for the crime.

"I know Thorpe, and I know he never did it. And I wondered. Then I read in father's book about that old tobacco pouch of mine being 'materialized.' So I knew there was trickery afoot. For I had handed that pouch to Kit only a short time before I fell down. And he hadn't handed it back. So, that accounted for its presence in the possession of the medium, though it didn't necessarily incriminate Shelby. He might have lost it or had it stolen from him.

"But, next I went to the Picture Show of 'Labrador Luck.' That, or at least the plot, the backbone of it, was

Blair's and mine. Together we doped it out, sitting by our camp fire up there in the wilds, old Kit dozing near by. He talked with us about it now and then, but his plans were different from ours. All for a monster, spectacular production which he has achieved, while Blair and I planned a little light comedy affair. But the plot, the great theme of the thing, was Blair's,—and I denounce Kit Shelby as the murderer of Gilbert Blair for the purpose of using that plot alone and in his own way! Another motive lay in the fact of his admiration for Carlotta Harper, whom, he thought, Blair was about to marry.

"And, if these do not seem to you, Mr. Weston and Mr. Wise, sufficient motive for murder, I will inform you that Blair had discovered Shelby's visits to the medium, Parlato, and had learned that it was he who was responsible for the tobacco pouch, the handkerchief and that forged letter. Blair discovered or suspected all this, and went to the medium and forced her to admit he was correct.

"Wherefore, Shelby had to be exposed and ruined, or—had to close Blair's lips forever. He chose the latter course. The method was by a poisoned soda mint, as has been suspected, and this I know, because Shelby and I talked over methods of murder, when we were discussing detective stories, and he detailed to me the very plan that I am sure he used himself, that of putting one poisoned pellet in a bottle of plain ones, and letting the result happen when it might. His argument was, that the murderer would be far from the scene at the time death took place. These statements I submit, and if Christopher Shelby can deny or refute them, none will be more glad than I."

Shelly maintained a sullen silence, refusing to look at Peter at all.

But Weston adjured him to reply to the accusations with either confession or denial, and he muttered: "Of course it's all true. I got in deeper and deeper and there was no way out but to do for Blair. I began giving the medium things just for fun,—the whole matter seemed to me such rubbish, and I never dreamed Mr. Crane would take it so seriously. Then when he did, and when Blair found out I had primed the medium, and when I wanted his play and he wouldn't let me have it, and when I wanted his girl,—and when he declared he would expose the medium business,—I fell for the temptation. That's all."

He lapsed again into utter dejection and Weston led him away before he should collapse utterly.

"Now, Julie, you can have your Mac," Peter went on, smiling at his sister. "It's too late to-night——"

"Not a bit of it," declared Penny Wise, "come along, Miss Crane, I'll take you to him, and let you tell him yourself, and I shouldn't be surprised if he came back with you."

The two went off joyfully, leaving Peter to be lionized and petted by his adoring people.

Madame Parlato had long since disappeared, being allowed to get away unmolested because of the help she had been.

Then Peter and his parents had a talk, while Carlotta just sat and looked at the group, knowing her turn would come. Zizi, too, like a little *dea ex machina*, sat, gloating over the outcome of it all.

Benjamin Crane utterly refused to listen to a word of regret at his discredited book,—he only laughed happily and declared it was a joke on himself, and he didn't care what the result might be or what loss he might suffer in reputation or in pocketbook.

Mrs. Crane said little but she held tight to the hand of her boy, and lost herself in an oblivion of happiness.

And then, turning to Carlotta, Peter said, "And you thought I'd never come back?"

"Peter," Carly said, "I'm an expert Ouija Boarder. I have the reputation of making the Board say whatever I want it to. But my own theory is, that the little pointer always goes straight to the message that the performer wants. And whenever I tried it alone, and asked it if you'd come back to me,—it said you would."

Peter smiled at her, a little quizzically.

"I don't know, Carly, whether you're making that up or whether you mean it, but it doesn't matter, I did come back,—and I came back to you,—and for you. Which, being interpreted, means, that when you're ready to go home, I'll walk along with you. I'll have time to see the family here to-morrow."

Whereupon Carly smiled happily, and they two "walked along."

THE END

Other Resurrected Press Mysteries From Carolyn Wells

A Chain of Evidence
Anybody But Anne
In The Onyx Lobby
Raspberry Jam
Spooky Hollow
The Clue
The Curved Blades
The Diamond Pin
The Gold Bag
The Man Who Fell Through the Earth
The Mystery Girl
The Mystery of the Sycamore
The Room With The Tassels
The Vanishing of Betty Varian
The White Alley
Vicky Van

Resurrected Press Mysteries From Louis Tracy

The Albert Gate Mystery
Four men murdered and a fortune in diamonds belonging to the Turkish Sultan stolen, while the Foreign Office official in charge has gone missing. Was it a common jewelry theft or was it a case of international intrigue? This is the question that barrister detective Reginald Brett must solve.

The Bartlett Mystery
When Ronald Tower is murdered on his way to a bridge game on the yacht Sans Souci it at first appears a common crime. But as Rex Carshaw finds, a tragic case of mistaken identity leads to political scandal among the rich and powerful of New York.

The Strange Case of Mortimer Fenley
When the wealthy Mortimer Fenley is struck down by a shot from an express rifle on the steps of his mansion, detectives Winter and Furneaux of Scotland Yard must find the culprit. Was it the artist who claimed he was painting a picture at the time of the shot? The disaffected younger son? Or is there another suspect?

The Stowmarket Mystery
For five generations the Fergus-Hume family has been cursed. Each of the baronets has met a violent end. When the fifth baronet is found slain by a ceremonial Japanese dagger, suspicion falls on his cousin David. It falls to barrister detective Reginald Brett to prove his innocence and find the real murder in a case that spans two continents and as many centuries.

Resurrected Press Mysteries by J. S. Fletcher

The Orange-Yellow Diamond
When an elderly pawnbroker is murdered in the London parish of Paddington, a young, down on his luck writer is accused of the crime. But then it's found the pawnbroker had had in his possession an extraordinary South African diamond worth over eighty-thousand pounds —a diamond that's now missing. It falls to Melky Rubenstein to unravel the mystery and prove the young man's innocence.

The Middle Temple Murder
When an elderly man's body is found on the steps of chambers in the Midde Temple, one of the Inns of Court, it falls to newspaperman Frank Spargo and Detective-Sergeant Rathbury to solve the crime. The murdered man, for indeed it was murder, was found with no money or identification on his person except for a piece of paper with the name and address of a young barrister. Who is the victim? Why was he killed? Who is the murderer?

Scarhaven Keep
Bassett Oliver, the famed actor, has gone missing. When Oliver fails to show for a rehearsal, aspiring playwright Richard Copplestone finds himself sent to the small village of Scarhaven on the northern coast of England to track down the actors movements. What he finds is mystery. Find the answers as Copplestone unravels the mystery of Scarhaven Keep.

Visit www.resurrectedpress.com

Resurrected Press Mysteries by Fergus Hume

The Green Mummy

Professor Braddock hoped to compare the burial practices of the Egyptians with those of the ancient Peruvians with his latest acquisition, the mummy of the last Inca, Caxas. But on arrival, the packing case proved to hold not the mummy, but the body of his assistant Sidney Bolton. It falls to Archie Hope to discover the murderer if he is to marry the professors step-daughter, Lucy Kendal. Who killed Bolton and where is the mummy? Was it the sea captain Hervey? The mysterious Don Pedro? Cockatoo the Polynesian servant? The professor, himself? And what has become of the emeralds? These are the questions that Hope must answer amongst the secrets of the past in The Green Mummy.

The Mystery of a Hansom Cab

"Truth is said to be stranger than fiction, and certainly the extraordinary murder which took place in Melbourne Friday morning goes a long way towards verifying that saying." Thus opens The Mystery of a Hansom Cab, the best selling mystery of the nineteenth century. When a man is found dead in a hansom cab one of Melbourne's leading citizens is accused of the murder. He pleads his innocence, yet refuses to give an alibi. It falls to a determined lawyer and an intrepid detective to find the truth, revealing long kept secrets along the way. Fergus Hume's first and perhaps most famous mystery... The Mystery Of A Hansom Cab.

Visit www.resurrectedpress.com

Resurrected Press Mysteries from the Dr. John Thorndyke Series

Dr. John Thorndyke Lecturer on Medical Jurisprudence and Forensic Medicine. Before Bones, before CSI, before Quincy, M.E– there was Dr. John Thorndyke solving the most baffling cases of Edwardian London using the latest tools of medical science. Read about his cases in:

The Eye of Osiris
John Bellingham, noted Egyptologist has vanished not once but twice in the same day. Now Dr, Thorndyke must unravel the tangled claims on his estate, solve the riddle of the missing man and find the "Eye of Osiris".

The Mystery of 31 New Inn
When Dr. Jervis is whisked away in a coach with no windows to an unknown location to treat a man in a coma from undivulged causes it is Dr. Thorndyke who must come up with the solution.

The Red Thumb Mark
The first of Dr. Thorndyke's cases finds him trying to prove the innocence of a young man accused of being a diamond thief despite the fact that his finger print was found at the scene of the crime.

John Thorndyke's Cases
More cases of medical mysteries as told by his trusted assistant Jervis, M.D. Eight stories of crime and deduction in Edwardian London.

Visit www.resurrectedpress.com

Resurrected Press Mysteries by John R. Watson & Arthur J. Rees

The Hampstead Mystery

High Court Justice Sir Horace Fewbanks found shot dead in his Hampstead home, a butler with a criminal past, a scorned lover and a hint of scandal. These are the elements of the Hampstead Mystery that Detective Inspector Chippenfield of Scotland Yard must unravel with the assistance of the ambitious Detective Rolfe. But will he be able to sort out the tangled threads of this case and arrest the culprit before he is upstaged by the celebrated gentleman detective Crewe. Follow the details of this amazing case at it plays out across Hampstead, London and Scotland until it reaches a stunning conclusion in the courts of the Old Bailey.

The Mystery of the Downs

When Harry Marsland was caught in a sudden down pour he sought shelter at Cliff Farm. Met at the door by a young woman clearly expecting someone else he is only too glad to get inside to wait out the storm. When they hear a noise upstairs in the deserted house they investigate only to discover the body of the farm's owner, Frank Lumsden, dead of a gunshot wound. Who then, killed Lumsden, and why? Who was the woman expecting and did she have any roll in the murder? These are the questions that private detective Crewe must answer in The Mystery of the Downs.

Visit www.resurrectedpress.com

Other Resurrected Press Mysteries

Mysteries on a Train

Before the Orient Express there was:

The Rome Express by Arthur Griffiths
A man is found dead in his first class sleeping compartment on the express from Rome to Paris. Who was his murderer? The Countess? The English General? His brother the clergy man? The maid who has disappeared? Is the French justice system up to solving the crime? Read about it in The Rome Express.

The Passenger from Calais by Arthur Griffiths
Colonel Basil Annesley finds he is the only passenger on the train from Calais to Lucerne. That is until a mysterious woman shows up at the last minute to book a compartment. Who is after her? What is her secret? Is she a criminal or a victim? Read about it in The Passenger from Calais

Visit us at www.resurrectedpress.com

About Resurrected Press

A division of Intrepid Ink, LLC, Resurrected Press is dedicated to bringing high quality, vintage books back into publication. See our entire catalogue and find out more at www.ResurrectedPress.com.

About Intrepid Ink, LLC

Intrepid Ink, LLC provides full publishing services to authors of fiction and non-fiction books, eBooks and websites. From editing to formatting, from publishing to marketing, Intrepid Ink gets your creative works into the hands of the people who want to read them. Find out more at www.IntrepidInk.com.